Triple Ripple

BRIGID LOWRY WAS born in New Zealand and lives in Perth. After the success of *Guitar Highway Rose*, she wrote *Follow the Blue*, and then she collaborated with her son, Sam Field, on the fantasy adventure *Space Camp*. Brigid's next novel, *With lots of love from Georgia*, won the Young Adult section of the New Zealand Children's Post Book Awards. Her collection of stories and poetry, *Tomorrow all will be Beautiful*, won the Victorian Premier's Award for Young Adult fiction and was shortlisted for the New Zealand Post Awards. Her inspiring guide for young writers, *Juicy Writing*, was a finalist in the New Zealand Post Awards.

Brigid teaches creative writing and also writes poetry and fiction for adults. She is in favour of op shops, travel, nectarines, coloured pencils and rivers.

BRIGID
LOWRY

Triple
Ripple

ALLEN&UNWIN

Allen & Unwin
83 Alexander Street
Crows Nest NSW 2065
Australia
Phone (61 2) 8425 0100
  Fax (61 2) 9906 2218
 Email info@allenandunwin.com
  Web www.allenandunwin.com

A Cataloguing-in-Publication entry is available from
the National Library of Australia www.trove.nla.gov.au

ISBN 978 174237 4994

Teachers' notes available from www.allenandunwin.com

Cover photo's by Getty Images / iStockphoto
Internal illustrations by Kim Fleming
This book was printed in December 2010 by McPherson's Printing
Group, 76 Nelson Street, Maryborough, Victoria, Australia

The paper in this book is FSC certified. FSC promotes environmentally responsible, socially beneficial and economically viable management of the world's forests.

10 9 8 7 6 5 4 3 2 1

'The writer provides one half and the reader the other.'
PAUL VALERY

And in the middle is the story...

THE WRITER

The writer lives in a house of many teapots.
Outside her window are roses and violets, and
cacti growing in old shoes. There are blue
mosaic steps that lead nowhere in particular.
The writer's world contains cake, cherries,
books, kind friends, and five pairs of slippers. It is a good life, yet the writer is not
entirely content. She struggles with reality,
despairing of the twenty-first century which
involves stuff she is not in favour of, such
as rampant capitalism, global warming, and
Botox. The writer is often more gloomy than
the situation demands. She struggles with
the hurly-burly of a world in which young
men drown and beloved dogs get run over. The
writer is kind of nuts, yet she's not nuts
enough to think that there actually _is_ a
place where no bad things happen. However,
she would prefer to live in a more elegant
world which has less suffering and more
happy bits in it. That's why she writes books.
She can't control the world, but on the page

she has supreme agency. Bad things still have to happen in a book, or else there would be no narrative, but at least in the world of words the writer gets to call the tune.

However, at present there's no tune. The writer is getting jumpy. People keep asking her what she's working on. For months she has mumbled excuses, but the longer she leaves it, the crabbier she becomes. Unless she wants to get a job in a supermarket, the writer must begin a new book.

An idea has come to her about a fairytale. It will have magic in it and some fairies, possibly goblins as well. Perhaps she will chuck in an amulet and some poison. It's time to begin.

CHAPTER ONE

T WAS SUMMERTIME when the girl Glory came to the palace; a time of honeysuckle and bees.

'Her mother was the seventh daughter of a seventh daughter,' said Mrs Blossom, the cook. 'But apparently the child has no magical powers, which is why she's been sent to us.'

'I heard her father drownded,' said Elda, the scullery maid.

'Yes, 'tis said he drowned,' sighed Mrs Blossom.

'I heard she has the reddest hair in all the nine counties,' added Alice, the garden girl, who'd just brought in a tray of peas and radishes.

Rolf, the kitchen boy, said nothing. He was busy watching a wasp struggle in a spider web.

'We'll find out soon enough, no doubt. Look lively, Lad. Them peas won't pod themselves.' Mrs Blossom heaved a mighty sigh and began rolling out a big lump of pastry on the cool marble table.

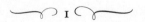

Those peas, thought Rolf. He was a boy of few words, but he knew how to use them. Mrs Blossom was a great one for misusing words, Rolf had observed.

'They might not put her in the kitchens with us, anyway, it's all theorezzical, but there are many places a lively girl could be useful round here. A palace doesn't run itself, you know. She might be in flowers with Miss Hope, or ... Get on with it, Rolf; stop dreaming, Boy.'

Please let her be in the kitchen with us, thought Elda. *Alice is all very well, but she doesn't have much laughter in her.* Elda liked the sound of a girl called Glory who had the reddest hair in all of nine counties.

Glory had always known it was her destiny to leave her home and family, but it had seemed a far-off thing.

'One day you shall go and live at the palace, as I did,' her mother had said, ever since Glory was a tiny girl. Now the time had come. She was to go and live in the royal palace and take employment there. At least she would be able to send home some coins to help her family. Life was pinch and scrape since Glory's father, a sea captain, had been lost in a storm, and she was much burdened by her mother's thinness and worry. Some evenings, the widow took only a crust, denying herself curd and broth so that Glory and her brothers might eat. She took in sewing, and the coal her sons collected brought in a few coins, but times were lean.

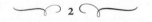

How Glory had loved her mother's tales when they were but fancy stories. Many was the long winter evening they'd sat by the hearth, darning socks, enjoying the warmth and the flickering dance of the flames, while Jakob and Ptolemy slept.

'You've been promised to the palace. It will be a great adventure for you, though many things will be different now. It is twenty long years since my time there.'

'Tell me, Mama.'

The widow's weary face softened as she drifted down the dusty corridors of memory.

'It is not a palace like a castle, made of stone and having moats, turrets and such things. It is a palatial mansion, with more rooms than you can count.'

'How many?'

'Eighty rooms or more. Two libraries, three kitchens, a grand ballroom, a star-gazing turret, and a small hospital. There are stately gardens with herbaceous borders, orchards, vines, a croquet lawn, vegetable gardens, a herb garden, gardens of flowers for picking to decorate the palace, and even topiary. It is a grander place than you could ever dream. It is a world within a world.'

'Topiary? Is that a beast like a horse, Mama?'

'Why would it be a beast? You are a funny girl, Glory. Topiary is the art of trimming trees into fantastic shapes, such as a giraffe or a teapot. The head gardener of my time, Mr Will, was a master of it.'

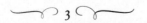

'You jest, Mama.' Trees cut into fancy shapes indeed. What silliness. Glory glanced around their humble cottage: an oak table, a stone fireplace, pots and pans, a closet for their clothes, two beds — one shared with her mother, one for her brothers. What, beyond this, would a person want or need? A little more food perhaps ... Surely her mother was spinning tales to make her laugh.

'You will see for yourself, Daughter, before too long. The grand ballroom has huge draperies of damask and crushed velvet, as ruched and fancy as ball gowns. On the afternoon of the grand balls, servant boys polish the dance floor by grating beeswax upon it, then sliding about with auld sacks on their feet, skating and laughing most joyous, despite the admonitions of the head butler, whose face, as I remember, resembled a shrivelled prune. I do believe those lads had more fun readying the dance floor than the dancers did in the evening.'

'It does sound wondrous indeed; this world within a world. Is the palace a happy place, then?'

A strange look came over her mother's face.

'It is a place like any other. You'll find good and bad there, as you find anywhere else.' Her tone was sharp, as if her daughter had spilt milk or forgotten to light the fire. 'Come now, Child. It's time for bed,' she continued, more gently.

Glory lay quietly, but sleep was a long time coming.

It was not the moon outside her window — round and yellow as the yolk of an egg — that kept her from slumber, but excitement. The very next day she was to travel far away, to live in a palace.

The Reader

》 Today had egg in it, and too much blue. It had Nigel Brown's smelly farts and Dylan Carmody's shitty behaviour. She is such a bitch to me. In Media she stuck a Post-it note on my back saying *Nova is a Poo Head*. I took it off straight away, but it was humiliating. I'm glad to be home, hiding in my room, reading my book. My mother gave me this one. I thought it would be crap because it's not my usual sort of book, although I liked fairy stories when I was little. I remember magic shoes and dancing swans that turned into princesses; Snow White and Rose Red; crotchety dwarves who turned straw into gold; enchantments and strange elixirs and dragons. I liked those stories because they were full of love and fear, and extraordinary things could happen.

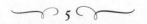

THE WRITER

It's easy to begin a book, inside your head. You start with a sparkly good idea. Then the real work commences. You create a place, an imaginative landscape, inviting the reader in. Then you add characters. Not boring ones. Your characters have to be interesting. The reader must turn the pages avidly to see what becomes of them. It's not enough to have a place and people. Things have to happen. One thing must lead to another. There have to be problems worth solving, and interesting adventures, big and small. Exciting, dramatic things are good in a story, but so are small, subtle things. If the writer thinks much more about this stuff, her head will explode.

She asks everyone she knows what a good fairy story should have in it. Tamsin says a pink princess. Sometimes it does not pay to ask Tamsin things. The writer lugs books home from the library and studies myths and legends. She doesn't want a troll in her book, because they are evil-tempered; nor a brownie, for they have no noses. But what if one sneaks in? The writer finds that the more she tries to think sensibly, the less her creativity creates. It's only during an afternoon spent on her bed, drinking tea, or in the middle of baking poppy seed cake, that her ideas arrive. The writer decides Tamsin was right about the princess, though perhaps not a pink one.

CHAPTER ONE AND A HALF

UEEN PETRONILLA HAD ordered Princess Mirabella to sort her jewels, but the princess was not in the mood. The peacocks were screeching horribly outside her window, and her chambermaid, Cherry, had a warty sore on her face. The princess could hardly bear to look at her. Furthermore, the peach on the princess's golden breakfast tray was as hard as a cannonball.

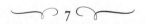

'You know my fruit must be ripe, Cherry.'

'I can't do nothing about it, Princess Mirabella. I just take what's given me by the kitchen. The kitchen just gives me what's given by the tree. If you isn't happy, I could bring you a napple.'

'I don't want an apple, you foolish creature. I want a juicy ripe peach, not a hard rock with fuzz on it. This peach just will not do.'

'Oh no, it just won't do. But there it is. I am so very sorry, Mistress.'

Cherry's tone was insolent, but she slinked from the room before the princess had time to reply. Mirabella would have liked to give her a good slap, but that wouldn't do either. She found it very hard being a princess. Life felt most unbearable.

Arlo, the page, brought her jewellery casket: a rosewood box inlaid with mahogany. It sat like a large, daunting frog, glaring at her. The princess felt grumpy about her mother's constant requests. As far as Mirabella was concerned, the queen had far too much time on her hands, especially when the king was away. She amused herself by ordering the staff about very energetically and concocting tasks for her daughter. Rarely did the princess wish to oblige, but this time she would obey; it was either that or stare out the window until she died of boredom. Oak, her horse, was being shod, so she could not ride. The long hours of the day hours stretched ahead like a dreary rope.

So she tipped the box, letting the contents tumble onto her cream silken coverlet. 'Twas a most fine coverlet, embroidered with roses and the royal crest, but made grimy by dust that had gathered amongst the royal jewels over the years. The princess saw by Arlo's haughty gaze that he considered tossing them down onto her bed a poor way to treat her jewels. He was quite handsome, Arlo, but he thought too well of himself, in Princess Mirabella's opinion.

'You may go,' she ordered, and he did. His shoes tapped all the way down the long corridor. Now that she was listening, she heard the sleepy buzzing of the bees in the hedge outside her window. A sweet sound, but overlaid by the cries of the infernal peacocks and — oh no, here was her mother, squawking even more annoyingly, if such a thing be possible. The queen was most displeased by the tangle on the bed.

'Oh, don't fuss, Mother. They're only things.'

'What do you mean, you stupid girl? How dare you treat your precious jewellery so carelessly?'

Princess Mirabella responded with silence, which oft proved to be the best way to lessen the wind in the royal sails. Queen Petronilla sighed mightily, then changed tack.

'This was your grandmother's wedding bracelet, you know. Amethyst carries the meaning of devotion.'

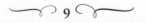

'Devotion. How amusing,' Mirabella muttered. Her grandparents had not been the happiest of couples. She'd heard the whispers about King Randolph's womanising ways and Queen Fortuna's fondness for wines and spirits — purely medicinal, you understand. Her mother's hearing was needle sharp. The princess should not have muttered thus, for now her mother was cross again.

'You will stay in your chambers until all the jewellery has been properly attended to. Set aside any pieces that need cleaning or mending. Try on each one carefully and select a necklace, with earrings to match. You must look your very best at the ball. I'll arrange for the tiaras to be brought to your chamber. We must see which one flatters your pretty complexion.' The queen tried to sweeten her daughter into compliance, which only served to annoy.

'Who cares about the stupid ball? I hate being paraded like a pony. You know I have no wish to make a match with any royal idiot, however great his fortune, however influential his parents.'

'You are a rude, ungrateful girl, and I am weary of your vexing ways. The king shall hear of it on his return.'

The Reader

⟩ I'm not sure where the story is going but I like books with a bit of mystery. Anyway, my book is more interesting than my life right now. School is dreary, and it's a great pity my mother didn't sort herself out a bit more before she decided to accept herself just the way she was. She pounces on me before I'm even halfway in the door. *Hello, Nova darling. How was school? Anything interesting happen?* I don't want to share my day. It's private. The other worst thing about my mother is how she's always trying to improve me: a little tidying here, a small suggestion there. Because Dad's away all the time, she focuses on me far too much. She can't allow me the dignity of being myself. I wish she'd accept that sometimes I'm grumpy and pessimistic, muddled and messy, lazy and lost. She should stop reading all those self-help books. They aren't doing her much good.

Dad is gone again. The house is strangely quiet. Mum's having a cleaning frenzy, and is snappy with me because she misses him. Go figure.

THE WRITER

The writer goes for her daily walk, hoping
for a line, a good thought, a solid idea, a
small miracle. She has no idea where her book
is heading. She urges herself not to panic,
but to get back to her desk. Sit down. Take
a breath. Write the next bit. Let the story
arrive.

CHAPTER TWO

HE DAY OF Glory's departure from the village
of Myddle Styx was a sad one. Her mother wept
softly, her brothers howled and snivelled, Glory
sobbed in noisy bursts. Even Mr Hobbs, the coachman,
blew his nose into his large red handkerchief.

'When will I see you again, Mama?'

'Try not to think like that, Chickadee. This is the
beginning of a great journey for you. Enter your new

life fully and don't look back. Courage, my beloved girl. All will be well.'

At that, Mr Hobbs gave his horse a great wallop, and they set off. Plum blossom fell dainty as snow as they travelled along the sunny riverbank, but it was not long before the dappled, leafy light faded and their carriage entered the gloomy woods. As her mother had instructed, Glory did not look back. There were no other passengers. Mr Hobbs sat like a giant at the front, and a load of boxes rattled and bounced on the wagon behind, as they tumbled onwards into the blackness. The fat moon rose. Glory fell asleep in a dreamy muddle of anticipation and fear.

At the palace, preparations for the grand ball were afoot. The invitations had been sent, the menu had been planned. The king and queen had arranged many suitors for Princess Mirabella to look at or, rather, many suitors to look at her. It wasn't true love her parents had in mind for their only daughter. In recent years the royal fortune had lessened considerably. There was the ill-fated battle in which they lost the river border, and the plague of locusts which decimated the wheat crop, but the main reason for their current predicament was that the king lacked the necessary skills for strong leadership. Easily flustered, he fumbled the affairs of state and lacked critical focus when it came to important decisions. If Mirabella could be married off to a rich prince from another kingdom, the royal fortune of the House of Hanover would be doubled. There'd be twice the army, twice the power. Princess Mirabella had no desire to be a pawn in this ancient game, but she saw no escape from it. The king had gone hunting, as usual, in order to avoid the queen's ranting about ruin.

'So I'm left here with these ridiculous baubles.' Mirabella sulked for a while, but then her vanity sneaked in on tiny rabbit paws. 'It will be the most horrid ball in the world, but I might as well look my best,' she decided. The princess set aside a necklace with a missing ruby, a teardrop earring without a partner, a sapphire and silver brooch which needed polishing. She tried on some necklaces but none of them appealed. Arlo delivered a towering pile of tiara boxes — eight of them — then lingered in the doorway.

'Yes? What is it?'

'It's Cherry, Milady. She's been taken ill.'

'I'm sorry to hear it. You can go now.' *Really*, she thought, *he is the most annoying person*. Fancy expecting her to be concerned about her maid's little troubles when she had these tiaras to deal with. The princess didn't bother trying them all on — it would have been too dreary for words — but she quite fancied the Razzle Dazzle Tiara. She twirled around in front of the mirror and found her reflection reasonably pleasing, yet perhaps she could do better? The Dancing Duchess Tiara was horribly heavy, the Blue Dream Tiara was far too big, the Stardust Tiara made her look like a wedding cake, the Wistful Rose Tiara had three rubies missing, and the Sugar-Plum Tiara was somewhat ordinary. The final box contained the Magic Blossom Tiara, which belonged to her eccentric Aunt Agatha, Duchess of Amberly. It was a delicate crown of diamonds and pearls set out in an intricate pattern of fleur-de-lis. It fitted perfectly, and the princess looked enchanting, but all this hard work tired her, so she decided to take a little nap.

CHAPTER TWO AND A BIT

THE KITCHEN WAS fragrant with vanilla and spices, for 'twas Tuesday, the day on which cakes and dainties were baked.

'Why is the queen so grumpy?' asked Elda. 'I heard there was fierce quarrelling, and that Princess Mirabella had been banished to her chamber.' Elda

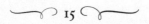

enjoyed nothing more than enlivening the kitchen with a scrap of gossip whenever she could.

'Maybe her crown is too tight?' Mrs Blossom believed a stupid question deserved a stupid answer. 'Best to keep your nose in your own business, Lass. Now get on with grinding those almonds; I need them for my cake.'

'Maybe a tiny insect flew into her ear and made a nest there?'

'Don't be ridiculous, Rolf.' Mrs Blossom was getting grumpy. Her legs ached, and now that she'd added the eggs, her butter and sugar mixture was starting to curdle.

'Maybe she isn't getting enough rumpty-tumpty?' offered Dirk, the beekeeper, who hadn't had any rumpty-tumpty himself for quite some time. Dirk loved to hang around the kitchen when he delivered the honey, for he didn't get to see womenfolk very often, spending his life on the road and in the fields, with only himself and the bees for company.

'Now, now,' clucked Mrs Blossom, but she couldn't help a smile. 'That's most pleasing honey you have brought me, Dirk. I'll make —'

But before she could speak of her plans for honey cakes and a new brew of mead, Mrs Blossom was interrupted by Arlo, pale of face and sombre of tone.

'There's been a tragedy, Mrs Blossom. Young Cherry is dead.'

The kitchen lurched to a halt in dreadful amazement. Mrs Blossom threw up her arms, knocking the poppy seeds into the cake batter, and dropped her rolling pin, not caring that it rolled under the table where Dirk's dog lay sleeping. Elda sobbed a loud unseemly sob, Dirk scratched his knobs by mistake, while Rolf stood silent with his mouth wide open.

'You'd best come with me, Mrs Blossom, for you are needed to help lay out the body..'

THE WRITER

She began with hope and glory, or rather with Mirabella and Glory, but now the wind has gone from the writer's sails. The whole idea of the book is slipping away from her like an elusive dream. She's just written two clichés in a row, which is a bad sign. The writer had only plotted the story to a certain point, and now that point has arrived. She wishes she knew the next bit, but she doesn't. Charles Dickens, when asked what would happen in the next day's instalment of <u>The Pickwick Papers</u>, replied that he didn't know, he hadn't written it yet. This is only slightly encouraging, since the writer is not Dickens and must travel alone, without a map, into the dark enchanted forest of her imagination.

The Reader

〉 Another crap day. Since Annie went to Sydney, I haven't had a close friend at school. I'm kind of a loner. I don't mind hanging out by myself, but I do mind Dylan. She calls me Nowhere instead of Nova, and sighs dramatically when I answer correctly in Lit. It pisses me off. I never did anything to hassle her, and she's got plenty of friends. I don't get it. Then Mum came home from work upset because they've changed her computer. She's worked at the Nursing Home for ages and usually she enjoys it, but she doesn't like learning curves, so it's mean streets at our house. Dinner got a bit burnt while Mum was on the phone whingeing to her sister. Our chops were edible, but only just. I shall shut the door on the world and read my book.

CHAPTER TWO
AND THE
NEXT BIT

THE COTTAGE WAS full of sorrow after Glory left. Jakob and Ptolemy pestered their mother all day long with endless questions.

'Why did Glory leave?'

'When will she come home to visit?'

The widow reassured them as best she could.

'You know she was always promised to the palace. Do not fret, my dears.'

She did not wish to burden her innocent lads with troubling shadows. When at last evening fell, she tucked her sons into bed, singing sad, sweet songs to them until they drifted into sleep. The unfriendly moon glared in the window, a cold, bright sliver offering no comfort. The widow knew her daughter's future was uncertain now, even more uncertain than the fragile lives of other mortals. She glanced at her boys again.

Yes, they were sleeping. She knelt beside her bed, but not to pray. Her fingers scrabbled for the stone she'd wedged so tightly all those years ago. Finally, she managed to dislodge it and take out the book. Its blue satin cover was ragged and stained. The widow rubbed the gilded, arcane sign of a star within a circle. She did not open the book. She was afraid to.

Mirabella dreamed of peacocks: peacocks in tiaras; peacocks in tiaras squawking up a storm.

'She's dead!' The queen towered above her, face milky white.

'What in heavenly blazes?' The princess was adrift between sleep and waking. Her mother's words made no sense at all.

'Your maid, Cherry. She has perished.'

'Don't jest, Mama. She was here this very morning, as usual, with my breakfast on a tray.'

'It is no jest. She was taken ill but hours ago, with most grievous frothing from the mouth and terrible jerking and twitching. She is dead. Nothing could be done to save her.'

Her mother's next words answered Mirabella's silent question: How can this be?

'She was bitten by a spider when gathering eggs several days ago, it seems, and has been taken more and more poorly ever since. Her body became covered with strange sores. Did you not notice anything?'

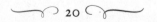

'There was a … a thing on her face today, Mama, but I thought nothing of it …'

'Come child, we must go. There is much to see to.'

By evening, Cherry's body had been bathed, the last rites had been administered, the family had been comforted, and the funeral had been arranged. Exhausted, Mirabella and the queen took refuge in the blue drawing room to discuss the need for a new maid. Finding a suitable one would be harder than it seemed.

'They are all quite wrong. Elda is scruffy and too timid. Alice is a bright lass, but her knowledge extends no further than cabbages and potatoes. She knows nothing of the ways of the royal chambers.'

'What about Molly, the niece of Mrs Blossom?'

'Don't be ridiculous. She is dimwitted.'

'Yes, it is rumoured she's not the full haystack. How about Veronica, daughter of the baker?'

'Shrill as a wasp.'

They sat in dull silence. What to do?

The Reader

❭ Today I felt beautiful and ugly all at the same time. Toby asked me to go skateboarding with him.

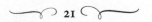

I said yes. We didn't skate much. Instead we kissed on a park bench. It was okay, but a bit too wet and tonguey. I didn't tell Mum about hooking up with Toby. When she asked if anything interesting happened, I pulled a silly face. That's not lying, is it? It's quiet around here while Dad is away. His job as a geophysicist takes him all over the world. It's not ideal, because a lot of the time there's just me and Mum. When Dad comes back we adjust to a life of threeness, but then he flies away again. My father loves his work, and even Mum has to admit that, because of the recession, it wouldn't be a great time for him to chuck in his job. So, for now, it's how we live. I've done my homework and washed the dishes. Mum's left for her sewing group, Stitch and Bitch, so I'm going to snuggle down and have a good old read. I wonder who the new maid is going to be, and why Glory's mother was scrabbling under the bed?

THE WRITER

It's going to be a big day today. Many things will happen. Time to set to work.

CHAPTER FOUR
AND THREE
QUARTERS

At first the journey provided a delightful array of new sights and sounds, but after three days and nights of hard travelling Glory was weary and sore. The bumpy ride seemed as if it would never end, and the inns they lodged in were of scant comfort, with hard beds, rough company, and strange noises in the night. The last day of passage was the longest, being nothing but uneven roads through plain farmland. Glory's head lurched up and down as she tried to sleep, tension clenching her forehead. Finally, on the fourth day, just as the evening light softened, Mr Hobbs announced that they were nearing the palace. Glory's spirits lifted. As they entered the driveway, Mr Hobbs gave his horse a light whip, and it trotted a little faster between rows of chestnut trees, towards the palace. What a grand sight! It was just as Glory's mother had said: a wondrous mansion with a thousand windows, dozens of tall chimneys, bright flags flying, and terraced lawns planted with lavender, peonies, and roses. A young man was chasing a small dog across the lawns. *I wonder who he is? And what a sweet little dog*, thought Glory. She could not wait to find out more about the world within the world.

'I'm to take you to Mrs Blossom in the kitchen, where you're to work. Once you are delivered safe and sound, I'll be on my way. I've a mind for an ale or two in the village tonight. Reckon I could put away a whole fowl, as well.'

Mr Hobbs's words faded into unimportance as soon as he mentioned Glory's job in the kitchen. How she wished he had told her earlier, for she'd done much imagining about her possible position. Scullery maid, chambermaid, laundry girl, assisting the seamstress... Glory had wondered about all of them and vowed that whatever came her way she would try her hardest to be a good worker and fit in to the life of the palace. The carriage came to a halt in a cobbled yard where a surprise was to be found. Standing outside the green door was a girl, with hair the colour of butter, sobbing most grievous into a ragged kerchief.

'What ails you, young Missy?' asked Mr Hobbs, as he got down and helped Glory to do the same.

'There's been a death,' the servant girl replied in

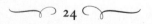

a shaky voice. She looked to be about twelve, a runty child with messy hair and a grimy hem dragging in the dust.

'A death?' Mr Hobbs spoke most serious. 'Not any of the royal family, I do hope and pray?'

'No, Sir. It were Cherry, Princess Mirabella's maid, Sir.'

'It's not a plague or a spreading sickness, now, is it?' Mr Hobbs took a few steps back and let go of Glory's hand very smartly. She felt more like a parcel now than ever before.

'No, Sir. It ain't the plague. Cherry took bad after a spider bite. She were gathering eggs in the hay barn when something bit her. It is said her blood were poisoned. First she were covered in sores, then this morning she fell to the ground and green foam frothed from her mouth, Sir.'

Mr Hobbs was in no need of this particularity of detail. He cleared his throat and became most businesslike.

'Where might we find Mrs Blossom, the cook?'

'She has duties, Sir, but I'm set here to wait for your arrival. I'm to tell you of the situation, and you are to leave the new girl with me.'

Mr Hobbs did not seem entirely sure about this arrangement, but after much scratching of his head and dabbing at his forehead he could think of no other.

'Be a good girl then, Glory, and do as you are told.'

He threw her small suitcase down, heaved himself up, and was gone.

'Come into the kitchen then,' said the girl. 'You must be Glory, which I think to be a lovely name. I'm Elda, the scullery maid.'

'Pleased to meet you.'

'Sit here. Are you hungry?'

'Yes.'

'Mrs Blossom said to give you this.' Elda pushed a cup of milk across the wide table, and a plate on which lay a slice of sweet cake dotted with tiny black seeds.

'What's this called?' Glory asked. 'It tastes delicious.'

Elda grinned and wiped the tears from her eyes. 'No wonder you haven't met it, for it didn't exist until today. Just after Mrs Blossom heard the dreadful news, she knocked the jar of poppy seeds into her almond cake. We're to call it Poppy Seed Cake. Mistake Cake, more like. I bet such things don't happen in the other kitchens here in the palace.'

'What are the other kitchens for?' Glory couldn't imagine why there would be a need for further kitchens, for she had never seen a kitchen as huge and splendid as this. There were gigantic marble chopping boards, and shelves stacked high with platters, bowls, tureens, pots, pans and cauldrons; there were sieves, ladles and graters dangling on hooks, and a row of wickedly gleaming knives was lined up on the bench.

'This kitchen is where we make the meals for the

royal family and the servants. Mrs Blossom came here as a scullery maid when she was a girl, and now she's head cook. She's kind enough, though it's always best to do as she says and be sharp about it. Beneath the tall chimbley is the bakery, where the daily loaves and buns are made. Be glad you don't work there, for the bowls are sticky and the tins are heavy, but worse than that is Mr Alfred, the head baker, who has wandering fingers, if you know what I mean. And then there's Miss Oleander's kitchen.'

'What's that one for?'

'They call it the magic kitchen, but it's just a joke. At least, I don't think Miss Oleander is a witch, but she *is* a strange woman. She's a herbalist and apothecary, who makes the royal medicines, cough syrups, and healing potions. Miss Oleander keeps to herself. No one is allowed in there without permission.'

'Oh,' said Glory, yawning. 'Couldn't the herbalist save Cherry?' The words spilt out before Glory had thought properly, and she hoped she had not said a wrong thing, but Elda answered her directly.

'If only she could have, but Miss Oleander was away picking herbs this morning. It all happened very fast, you see. Cherry had a few sores and felt poorly, but she were walking around, until she weren't.'

'Oh.' Glory yawned again. Her eyelids wouldn't stay open.

'Come on. Bring your bag, and I'll show you where we sleep.'

'This is the servants' quarters,' explained Elda, once they had crossed the courtyard and entered a tall brick building on the far side. It had three levels, and as the two girls climbed the winding wooden staircase they passed many doors painted in bright colours.

'The groomsmen and junior male servants' rooms are on the first floor. The senior staff live on the second floor. We're not allowed to go in any rooms that ain't ours,' explained Elda. 'Me and you are in the attic, right at the top. Right here, in fact. Cherry slept here, but her belongings have been given back to her kinfolk.'

An uncomfortable silence followed.

'Don't worry, she didn't die here. She died in the laundry room,' Elda explained.

Not sure what else to do, Glory offered a quiet smile, and Elda returned it. Their attic was a narrow room with a window, a faded green rug, two shelves, and just enough space for two cots and a washstand. From the window, Glory saw peacocks strutting on the velvety lawn, and ducks floating in the moat. Muslin curtains fluttered in the evening breeze.

'This is your bed, and this is your shelf. We share the chamber-pot what's under here.' Elda blushed with embarrassment.

'Don't worry. I'm not a fussykins. I'm used to such things. It's a fine room and, as far as I know, I'm not a snorer. We'll do all right together, us two.'

'We don't have no duties tonight, but we start

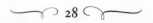

sharp at six so we might as well get some sleep.' Elda took off her faded leather shoes, and Glory began to unpack her few belongings.

In the tavern late that night, Mr Hobbs, the carrier, wiped his chin.

'An excellent supper. Most excellent indeed.'

Dirk, the beekeeper, nodded in agreement. The two men, hitherto strangers, were friendly fellows now, having shared several tankards of dark ale and a hearty meal of boiled fowl, turnip, cabbage, and pease pudding.

'I left the girl at the palace, as I were supposed to. I'll load my cart with hay, oil and wines, and make my way back to Myddle Styx when dawn breaks on the morrow.'

'You know about her mother and the curse, no doubt?' Dirk scratched his beard in a troubled manner, for there were many fleas in the straw at The Fat Pig Inn.

'Women's mumbo jumbo,' declared Mr Hobbs. 'I've no time for such nonsense.'

Dirk said no more. There are those who believe in magic, and those who do not. The beekeeper knew more than he wished to about such things, but there was no point wasting his words on an unbeliever. Nor did he mention the sudden unusual shadow that passed across the waning moon. Mr Hobbs was quite oblivious, being much engrossed in the sight of the ample, creamy bosom of the serving girl delivering the tankards.

THE WRITER

It's easy to let a whole day slip by. The writer's kitchen cupboard is overflowing with plastic containers, mainly from supermarket hummus. Wanting to help save the planet, the writer goes to buy an avocado, instead, to spread on her toast. Hours later, she's bought a new pair of shoes and a black pen, hung out in the library looking for books about magic, and visited several op shops. 'It's almost time for afternoon tea. I'll make a cuppa and set to work,' says the writer, and then the phone rings. 'What a fine thing an avocado is; a perfect creamy spread in its own organic, biodegradable container,' she tells her friend on the phone. Her friend says the writer needs to get out more. Staying home alone does not seem to be good for her mental health. 'Actually, I've been out all day! Better do some work! Okay, see ya,' says the writer. She'd better crack on. Glory hasn't even met Mirabella yet.

The Reader

⟩ That's weird. Mum brought home a slice of gorgeous lemony poppy seed cake for me—and while I was eating it, it got invented in my book. Spooky. She's gone to bed with a headache, leaving me instructions to fold the laundry and sort out the recycling, but I can't be bothered. I'm over global warming. It seems to me that the planet was pretty much rooted before I got here. Now I'm supposed to fix it. I want a t-shirt that says: *Decline of Planet Not My Fault*.

ANOTHER
CHAPTER

A T DAWN, WHEN THE roosters began to crow, Elda shook Glory awake. They washed their faces in the white china bowl and hastened to the kitchen. Glory was taken by surprise when she saw the size of Mrs Blossom. The name was so pretty she hadn't expected the cook to be a mammoth sow of a woman with arms as hefty as hams, and a hairy chin. Mrs Blossom looked Glory up and down, turned her around, and sighed fit to knock down a haystack.

'I could have done with you, Lass, in my kitchen. But you are to become Princess Mirabella's maid.'

Alice gave a big happy shout.

'Thank goodness it were not me. I have been so afeared of it.'

'Nor me,' added Elda.

'Why not?' Glory asked. 'Surely to be the maid of a princess is a good thing?'

'You ain't met the princess,' said Alice.

'She have a very bad temper on her,' added Elda.

'Quiet, you two,' Mrs Blossom bellowed. 'That's enough! Rolf, take her to the princess's chambers and come straight back. No skedadling into the garden or linky-lanking in the corridors. I need you to wash the leeks.'

Glory liked the look of Rolf. He was tall and skinny, with kind eyes and a gentleness about him. She returned his welcoming smile with a question.

'I saw you yesterday, as I arrived, chasing your wee dog. Did you manage to catch it?'

'Eventually. But she's not mine. That was Arabella, the queen's beloved pet. She's a bundle of mischief, a veritable minx, and often runs away.'

'I've never had a pet, unless you count the hedgehog that lived beneath our cottage. It must be grand fun.'

The young man led the way along long corridors lined with family portraits in heavy gilded frames. Rolf stopped beneath one of the paintings.

'This is Prince Oscar. He's my favourite. He studied all the courtly arts: languages, music, poetry, botany. He was an adventurer, too, but he died young.'

'What happened to him?' asked Glory. The young man in the portrait did seem a most agreeable fellow, with his smiling eyes and dashing grin.

'He died in strange circumstances.'

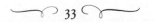

'Like what?'

'No one knows, or at least I don't. His mother, Agatha the Duchess of Amberly, went completely mad after his death, they say. There are quite a few secrets in this palace, if you want my opinion.'

Glory wanted to know about secrets, but even more urgently she wanted to know something else.

'Is Princess Mirabella really so horrible?'

'May I give you some advice?' Rolf replied. 'If it were me, I would treat her like a bad-tempered horse. I wouldn't take too much nonsense, and I would only give her a sugar lump when she behaved herself, if you understand me.'

'I do,' laughed Glory. 'Thank you, Rolf.'

'Come on, I'd better deliver you there, and get back to the kitchen before Mrs Blossom worries herself into a puddle.'

The pair scurried along the corridors until they came to a vast mahogany door carved with the royal crest. Rolf rang the bell.

'Enter,' came a muffled command.

'Good luck. Remember there's always company to be found in the kitchen.' Rolf winked, then turned and ran.

At first it was hard to see anyone, for the room was so grand and so full of fancy things. Green birds decorated the pale blue wallpaper, lacquered screens danced with dragonflies, yellow roses and orange peonies spilt from vases, and the carved bed was hung with damask curtains and turquoise tassels. Glory's first thought, when she saw Princess Mirabella, was that she was as beautiful as an angel. Glory's second observation was that it was a grumpy angel, because the royal face wore a fierce scowl. Glory's next feeling was one of puzzlement, because the princess was wearing only a white lace petticoat, pulled up above her knees, and her feet were stuck in a large, blue, floral china tureen.

'I suppose you're Gloria, my new maid. Well, it took you long enough to get here. Don't stare. Haven't you ever seen anyone enjoying a footbath? Hurry up and dry my feet. My page brought this water ages ago. It's completely cold.'

'My name's Glory, actually.'

'I don't care if your name is Petal Nectarine Rainbow. Dry my feet, and hurry up about it.'

Glory did as she was told. She was amazed that the two royal feet needed so much attention. They were dutifully dried, massaged with a balm of rose petals and lavender, then carefully tucked into pink silk socks and green satin slippers.

'How was your first day?' Elda asked, when the two girls were tucked up in bed that night.

'The princess has a very nasty manner. She treated me most rudely.'

'Yes, they say she was born sour. Came into this world with a frown on her tiny, wrinkled face, and has made a habit of discontentment ever since. Some of the stories Cherry told us would make squirrels die of fright. The only thing Cherry liked about being Princess Mirabella's chambermaid was that it meant she got to see Arlo. He's a nice looker, that one. Lord, my feet are tired. We stewed pears today, a huge vat of them. I don't care if I never see another pear ever again.' Elda snuggled down, and her breathing soon softened into sleep.

Glory lay silent. How she wished to be at home, in the quiet cottage, with her beloved mother and brothers. A huge wave of longing overcame her as she recalled the dappled firelight and the comfort of her mother's voice, so very far from this unfamiliar world and narrow, lonely bed. A funny little tear drop ran down her nose by mistake. *Never mind*, she consoled herself. Perhaps tomorrow all would be beautiful.

The next morning, a funeral was held for Cherry in the chapel. Her mother, plump as a pudding, could not contain her grief, and sobbed all through the ceremony. Her father stood steady until the slender coffin, draped with honeysuckle, was carried out by four lumbering local lads, and then he wept in great gasping sighs, his chest heaving like a boat in a rough ocean. Afterwards, the servants gathered in the courtyard for ale and sweetmeats, standing in quiet groups, clumsy with sorrow. The queen and the princess withdrew to the royal chambers and drank port wine from tiny glass goblets. Mirabella was subdued. She felt as if she'd been punched. How shallow things seemed, in the face of death.

'I wish your father were here. His support in times of need is sadly lacking.'

'Yes, Mama.'

'But I think we have managed the funeral well enough. Do you not agree?'

'Indeed, Mama.'

'But the king will be home before long, and then there is the ball to look forward to.'

Mirabella turned her head away, knowing this would be a poor time to speak of her feelings about her future.

Each new day, Glory hoped for smoother times, but it was not to be. The princess was petulant when her fruit was not perfectly ripe, sulked when her egg wasn't boiled correctly, snarled if her hair wasn't brushed gently enough, and became grumpy when her riding boots weren't polished to her satisfaction. It was 'Do this', 'Do that', from dawn until dusk, with never a 'Please' nor a 'Thank you'. On the fourth day, after the princess had eaten her breakfast of porridge, pears and clotted cream, she instructed Glory to fetch her finest gowns so she might choose an outfit for the ball.

'Lay them on the bed.'

Glory took the first gown from its silk wrapping and placed it gently on the bed.

'Not like that. Do it properly. You'll rip them if you aren't more careful. Were you born in a barn, you clumsy creature?'

'No, I was born in a cottage, where people had manners.'

'How dare you speak to me like that? Apologise at once!'

'I shan't. I've had enough of your tantrums. If you want me to be your maid, you must treat me respectfully.'

'I beg your pardon?'

'You heard me.'

'Get out of my sight!' The princess stamped her foot so hard it made her wince with pain, but Glory felt no sympathy. She turned and left.

Rolf was sitting on a wooden stool in the sun, outside the kitchen, shelling almonds.

'Hello,' he said. 'What's the matter? You look very pale.'

'I am pale,' said Glory, sitting down beside him. 'Pale with rage and fury. You know that advice you gave me regarding the princess? Well, it didn't work. She never acted nicely enough for me to give her a sugar lump. In fact she treated me so rudely that I was insolent to her. She has kicked me out.'

'I told you she was a bad-tempered horse. Kicking the chambermaid, that's awful. A horse should know better.'

'It isn't the least bit funny, Rolf. I'll be sent home in disgrace, without any wages. I wanted to do well here, to make my mother proud of me.'

Before Rolf could answer, Arlo appeared. His satin breeches were perfectly fitted; his black leather shoes had big brass buckles, and shone like treacle.

'The queen wants to see Glory. At once. In the blue drawing room.'

'I told you so.' Glory stood up, a bit shakily.

'Stay steady. I'll be waiting.' Rolf said, but even he looked doubtful.

The Reader

》 I wonder why Glory was sent to the palace. It's related to the magic book under her mother's bed, no doubt. I wonder how the writer thinks all that stuff up? It must be quite hard having to come up with original ideas. I don't think I'd like to be a writer. I'm thinking of becoming an architect, a web designer or a florist. I would also like to travel the world, helping people and having adventures in interesting places.

THE WRITER

The writer has come to a big decision. There are to be no fairies in her book, and this is why: she doesn't believe in fairies. She doesn't <u>not</u> believe in them, either, but she's never seen one or felt one near. She likes the idea of them, and has nothing against small children wearing gauzy floaty costumes. But no actual fairy has ever come to the writer's house, nor done a fairy thing to her. She does believe in invisible forces, though.

CHAPTER
SEVENTEEN AND
THRUPPENCE

THE QUEEN WAS wearing a purple gown with an ermine collar, and purple satin slippers with ermine trim. Arabella lay sleeping on her lap. Glory stood nervously before Her Highness, waiting for the worst to happen, but the royal greeting was surprisingly pleasant.

'Sit, Child. Would you care for some tea?'

'No thank you, Ma'am.' Glory knew her hand would tremble if she held a teacup. She wished she had a dear little dog, gentle upon *her* lap. Stroking such a soft creature would surely soothe and calm her. The queen took a sip of tea and fiddled with the dainty cake before her.

'Princess Mirabella has told me what happened

between you. I'm disappointed to hear it, though not entirely surprised. My daughter has never been an easy person, and her maid's sudden death has unsettled her. However, I do not approve of rudeness; not from the princess, nor from my servants. Do you understand me?'

Glory nodded.

'Good. There will be no more discourtesy, and you will perform your work calmly and cheerfully. I shall give you other duties for a week. On Monday morning you'll resume your station as royal chambermaid, when I expect the two of you to make a fresh start.'

'Thank you, Ma'am.' Glory wasn't sure if she was happy to hear the news, or sad, but on balance this plan seemed preferable to being sent home in disgrace after only four days.

'Arlo will show you to the library, where you will dust all the books and all the shelves. When that's done, Mrs Blossom is expecting you in the kitchen. Alice, the garden girl, was called home yesterday. Her father is purported to need her, but it is more likely a reaction to the news of Cherry's illness. I am not happy about it, but...'

The queen's voice trailed off, and she rang her bell to summon the page, then turned her attention to Arabella, who'd woken up and seemed to be choking on a cake crumb.

'So?' Arlo asked eagerly, once they were out of earshot of the queen.

'I'm on other duties until Monday, when I shall resume my post as Mirabella's maid. I have been instructed to be politeness itself, which I shall attempt.'

'Interesting,' said Arlo. 'Here's the library, which you'll find very peaceful after Mirabella's hoity-toity ways. The duster is in the cupboard.' He smiled winningly, then strutted away. *What a peacock*, thought Glory. *He's very handsome, but the effect is ruined by his own good opinion of himself.*

It was a magnificent library. Books lined the walls from floor to ceiling, and light bathed the room through leadlight windows, creating diamond patterns on the polished floor. Glory took up the feather duster and set to work, yet she made slow progress, for each book was a doorway to a world of mystery and amazement. *What a lovely punishment*, thought Glory. *A library is a type of paradise for me.* She recalled the pleasure of being taught to read by her father, and the happy times she'd spent reading folktales to her brothers. Glory waved her duster like a magic wand, then continued her work. She took each book down, dusted it carefully, then opened it to look inside. She was deeply absorbed in the travels of a Spanish explorer when gradually she came to have a feeling she was being watched. Maybe there were ghosts in here. *Come now, don't be a dandelion head*, she told herself, but the feeling grew stronger rather than weakening. Slowly, Glory turned around and saw a woman standing in the doorway, watching her intently; a woman of faded beauty, with olive skin and deep blue eyes. Her silver-flecked dark hair was tied in a knot, and she wore a grey gown embroidered with stars. Neither spoke for a long moment.

'So you are Glory? They told me you'd arrived, but I wanted to see you for myself. It's true, you are here at last. My name is Persia Oleander.'

'Hello,' said Glory, for she could think of no other reply. The woman had a unsettling intensity about her.

'Do you know who I am?'

'Elda told me that . . . you're the court herbalist. You keep your own kitchen and make the royal medicines, so she said.'

'Is that all you know of me?'

Glory nodded, unwilling to voice the other things Elda had said, especially the magic part.

'Your mother did not mention me?'

'No,' Glory replied, puzzled.

'Is she well, my old friend Rosamund?'

'Fairly well, though she gets weary from caring for my brothers and the house, and from the work she takes in.'

'If you make a visit home, I shall brew her a tonic. We were very close, Rosamund and I, when she lived in the palace.'

'Oh,' said Glory, not knowing what else to say, but it did not matter for the woman had turned and disappeared.

After dinner that evening, in the candlelight of the queen's chambers, Mirabella recounted her version of the incident with Glory.

'... the rudest of replies, and then she stormed out. It was unpardonable, Mama. You must send her home immediately!'

'I shall not. Glory is to remain in royal employ. After a period of other duties, she will be given another chance as your maid.'

'But *why*, Mama?'

'There are reasons for this that I am unable to share with you, Mirabella. However, let me remind you that graciousness and good manners are always appropriate for a princess.'

'I may have been a smidgin high-handed, but the girl lacks the necessary humility for a servant's position, in my view.'

'Mirabella!'

'Oh all right, Mama. I suppose we can see how it goes when she returns to my service. She's a pretty thing, I admit. Her hair is such an unusual shade of red, somewhere between a summer plum and the loudest sunset.'

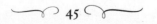

The queen closed her eyes and sighed. Mirabella sighed, too. She had ridden that morning, which was all to the good, now that Oak was returned to fine fettle. The princess loved riding. Galloping across the meadows, alone with her beloved horse, was the nearest she ever got to freedom. However, the rest of Mirabella's day had been sheer tedium. She'd spent the afternoon staring out the window, watching Elda picking rosehips in the walled rose garden. Since Cherry died, Mirabella had been feeling even more not-knowing-what-to-do-ish than before.

'Perhaps I could attack a peacock with my diamond hairpin,' she whispered, but she need not have bothered whispering because the queen had fallen into a right royal slumber.

THE WRITER

The most interesting thing that's happened to the writer lately is losing her purse and then finding it again. Things are a little more complex in her book, though. She was going to have Glory's mother explain about Miss Oleander, and the magic that went wrong, and what happened to Prince Oscar. But she remembered that Dickens said, 'Make them laugh and make them weep but above all make them wait.' So she has changed her mind.

The Reader

〉 Toby and I went to the park after school. For no actual reason, I didn't like him anymore. His jeans were so baggy and hung so low they looked ridiculous. When he tried to kiss me, I said I had a sore throat, then I pretended to remember that I had to pick up some knitting stuff for Mum. 'Whatever,' he said, which seemed ridiculous, too. I'm turning into a nerdy girl who'd rather read a book than kiss a boy in a park.

A BIT THAT IS TOO SMALL TO BE A CHAPTER

GLORY COULDN'T SETTLE after Miss Oleander's strange visit. Somehow, the books no longer held the same interest for her, which meant she worked faster, clearing the shelves of books, dusting each one, wiping down the shelf and returning the volumes in tidy rows. Glory was much puzzled. Why had her mother not told her about the apothecary, if they had been such good friends? It was very odd. When the clock struck noon, the hungry girl hastened down the back staircase to the kitchen, which smelled of meaty deliciousness.

'Still with us, Missy? Well, 'tis a lucky day for you and a lucky day for me as well, for I need all the help I can get here, and how I'm expected to manage without Alice I just don't know. Her father said he needed her to look after a sick pig. I never heard of such a feeble excuse!' Mrs Blossom resembled a snowstorm, her dark hair dusted with flour. 'Servants' lunches is barley broth and soda bread. Take it outside to eat. I'm busy as a basket here and I don't want no ones and nuffinks underfoot.'

Glory sat on the bench and ate her lunch by herself. She hoped that Rolf would come, but he didn't. Back in the library, she resumed work. With a reluctant sigh, she began dusting the history books which occupied the highest shelf. She climbed the small ladder, then lifted each heavy volume with one hand and dusted underneath it with the other. It was sneezy work, and it took quite a bit of skill to balance, lift, dust and replace without toppling onto the floor. As Glory lifted the last book on the last shelf, she paused. The book was much too light. She climbed down and opened it, only to find that the pages had been cut out to form a box.

The Reader

⟩ I'm not going to get a chance to read tonight. Too much homework. Dylan was a bitch again today. She hid my backpack. It took me ages to find it. When I finally managed to locate it, under the steps, she was standing nearby, sniggering, so I know it was her. Tara reckons it's because D has a major crush on Toby, and she heard that I dumped him. You would think that would have pleased her but, no, apparently not. School is not my favourite place right now, I'll tell you that for free. One fun thing happened, though. My art teacher showed me a glossy magazine with a painting that has the best-ever title: 'I'm not doing a poo today because I'm wearing blue eye shadow and a crown.' Very, very cool. I wish the world was more fruity. I wish we all wore crowns, and tiaras, and strange hats. I'd like a green velvet hat with stars and diamonds on it. Regarding hats, my mother is knitting me a beanie. She's using nice wool: purple, blue, green, yellow, orange and red, to make funky rainbow stripes. But I'm worried it's going to come

out all scrunchy, and blobby, and weird in a bad way.
Mum's really missing Dad. She's eating too much
chocolate and keeps getting up off the sofa to tidy
things. Funny old world. Funny old Mum.

THE WRITER

The writer is going away for a while. Her life
has become a scramble of emails, errands, and
obligations. There are many Urgent Things
That Must Be Done Before Leaving. She would
like to stay home, in her quiet house of teapots. Travel is unsettling, and the logistics
are tricky. Travelling light is a foreign
concept for the writer, who wishes to take
two pairs of slippers, a cosy rug, a stash of
good tea, a bar of dark chocolate, an umbrella,
a raincoat, a warm coat, a meditation stool,
soap that smells fabulous, a journal, three
books, two pens, some coloured pencils, a warm
hat, a scarf, at least three pairs of shoes
but possibly seventeen, jeans, boots, skirts,
tops, dresses, an orange petticoat, jewellery,
a nail file, a tiny Buddha statue, and a collection of gifts for friends. Now she has no

time to write, and she is worried. What if she loses the plot completely and can't find her way back into her story when she gets to the new place? Before she leaves town, she has to get Glory out of that frigging library; the poor girl's been stuck there for days. And what on earth is going to be in that box? A feather, a stone, a letter, a bloodstained handkerchief, a ballet slipper, a partridge in a pear tree...

The Reader

⟩ I've been sad today, for no particular reason. If wet weather, a neurotic mother, an absent father, knobbly knees, too much homework, and poxy skin don't count as reasons, that is.

I'm too tired to keep reading. I keep dropping the book, and tomorrow looms, with double maths, sport and all sorts of bizzy whizzyness. I do hope Glory...

A CHAPTER WITH A BAD MISTAKE IN IT

THE BOOK THAT was really a box contained three yellowed photographs. The first was of a tree. The next was of two young women wearing pale dresses, standing in a garden. 'That's Miss Oleander and my mother,' Glory whispered in amazement. The last photograph was of a young man. Glory looked at him long and hard because, although it made no sense, the handsome youth seemed familiar. She leapt to her feet, shoved the book with the secret compartment back on the shelf where it belonged, tucked the photos into her apron pocket, and dashed down the corridor. Taking a wrong turn, she ended up in a vast room of ghostly chairs draped in dust covers. Glory sprinted back the way she'd come. She hurried to the end of the next corridor, then dashed to the right, down the long hallway that led towards the kitchen, stopping beneath the portrait of the handsome young prince.

She held up the photograph. Yes, it was definitely him: Prince Oscar. Glory walked slowly back to the kitchen, but there was no time to think for she was promptly set to work.

'Finished dusting them books? I can do with you here, Missy, make no mistake about it. I've run out of onions, and the queen has asked for cream of onion soup. Go down into the cellar for me and fetch some, there's a good girl.'

Mrs Blossom smiled, and Glory went to get the onions. She was keen to look at the photos again, but she didn't want to get into trouble.

'Tonight,' the girl promised herself. 'When Elda goes to sleep, I'll have a proper think. It'll be quiet then and I'll be able to make sense of things.'

THE WRITER

The writer has finally written the bit that gets Glory out of the library. It feels most satisfying. She goes walking in the wild wind, alive to inside-out umbrellas, wet roses, a cat in a window, an almost invisible rainbow. It is a joyous day indeed, but then... The writer

hurries home and turns on her computer, then
googles. When was photography invented? 1932.
Bugger. She starts again.

A CHAPTER WITHOUT A MISTAKE IN IT (HOPEFULLY)

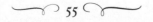

THE BOOK THAT was really a box contained a
letter, but there wasn't time to read it because
right then Arlo stuck his head around the corner.

'Get down to the kitchen at once. Mrs B is having
a fit.'

Glory hurried downstairs, where she was promptly
pounced on by a frazzled Mrs Blossom.

'Duke and Duchess Ditchling are coming to dinner,
and the queen wants my cream of onion soup, and roast
meat, and goodness-knows-what tonight, and all at the
last minute. Hurry down to the cellar and get me the

big bundle of onions hanging on the back of the door. Look smart about it.'

'The cellar?'

'No, the bleedin' elephant's trunk! Has your brain turned into a pumpkin? Down t'stairs on t'other side of courtyard. Get going, Girl, don't stand there like a chimpamzee.' Mrs Blossom's bosoms shook like two vast jellies.

The cellar was a treasure trove of edible delights and wondrous smells. There were smoked hams and sausages dangling from the ceiling, baskets of dried mushrooms, stone tubs of chutneys and pickles, fat rounds of cheese, bunches of dried bay leaves, sage and thyme, and kegs of ginger beer.

Glory would have liked to linger in this spicy place, but remembering Mrs Blossom's heaving bosom she tried to recall her task. There were too many new things in her fuddled brain, especially the matter of the book that was really a box, and the letter. Onions! That was it! She grabbed a large bunch and sped back to the kitchen. Mrs Blossom barely looked up from the huge haunch of venison she was studding with sprigs of rosemary.

'Good girl. Now peel 'em and slice 'em thinly, then put 'em into that big, black pot with the leeks and garlic what Rolf has already prepared. Where is that dratted boy? I sent him to find Elda, who went to pick fresh herbs, and now they've both vanished. How shall

I get this dinner done with only you to help me?'

Glory set to work. The knife was sharp, and she worked steadily. Mrs Blossom seemed pleased.

'I don't know where them others is, so I'm putting you in charge of the soup. Fry the onions slowly in butter to gentle the flavours. Don't let them burn, mind you. When they're golden, add that jug of chicken stock and simmer until the onions melt into the broth. Take it off the heat, sieve it, and add this bowl of fresh cream. Taste it and season with salt and plenty of nutmeg, there's a lamb.' Mrs Blossom returned to her work, cracking eggs into the buttery batter in her pudding bowl. For three and a half minutes there was peace in the kitchen.

'Holy Trout! What's on earth's happened to you?' bellowed Mrs Blossom.

Elda stood in the doorway, her face badly swollen.

'I've been stung by a bee that flew out of the raspberries.' Elda's voice was faint and raspy.

'Her throat is swelling. She's having trouble breathing.' Rolf stood by, terrified.

'Take her to Miss Oleander. She'll know what to do. Oh dear, she do look unwell. I'll come with you. Steady now, Elda, you're going to be all right. Glory, stay here and make that soup, just like I told you.'

The Reader

❭ My mother is particularly cranky, even for her. *Nova, clean your room. Nova, finish your homework. Nova, do your piano practice. Nova, turn your music down, I have a headache.* She always has a headache. I want to live all by myself on my own planet with a white cat called Whizzbang and a goldfish called Gizmo.

THE WRITER

The writer flies across oceans and lands in her new location. At first it feels more like dislocation. Her body arrives, but her mind is muddled and undone. The soul travels at the pace of a camel, so the Arab proverb goes. She unpacks her red suitcase. She walks a lot, tasting the sights and sounds of the new place. She buys flowers to brighten her room, and gypsy earrings. She sets up her computer, hoping the muse will be able to find her. The writer fidgets a lot, eats a lot, and refuses to answer people who ask how the book is going because, to quote a proper famous writer, 'Talking about your novel while you're writing it is like opening the door when you're cooking a soufflé.' But it would be good to get some advice from the Goddess of Wonderful Writing, because the writer realises that Glory shouldn't have found a <u>letter</u> in the box. It's predictable and boring. She wanders aimlessly around the new city, idling the days away. At night, she dreams about her father, dead since she was a girl. She dreams about frozen pansies, a band called the Wobbly Jellies, a tree house with a library in it. One night, a girl comes riding a bicycle into her dreams. The writer recognises her. It is her reader. A kindred spirit for whom she must continue her story. 'Damn,' she says. 'Now I'll have to keep writing this book, despite all my fears and hesitations. A girl is waiting to read it. As for my dead father... well, if I can't have a real father, at least I can enjoy creating some imaginary ones.'

A CHAPTER
WITHOUT A
BORING BIT IN IT
(HOPEFULLY)

LORY SAT DOWN on the floor. The book that was really a box was empty. How strange it was. Why would anyone go to the trouble of making a hiding place and then not hide anything in it? It didn't make sense. Just then Arlo stuck his head round the corner.

'Get downstairs at once. Mrs B is having a fit.'

When Glory arrived in the kitchen, she was promptly pounced on by a blathering Mrs Blossom.

'The king's coming home tonight. His aide rode in to give warning. The queen's ordered cream of onion soup, roast venison and fig pudding. She's got no idea, that woman. Thinks I'm a magician wot can produce hurricanes and miracles. Hurry down to the cellar and fetch me some onions.'

'Where's the cellar?'

'Down t'stairs on t'other side of courtyard. Don't stand there like a rhinocerump.' Glory's brain was a mess of wobbly clouds. There were too many new things in it. She was especially perplexed about the empty book. The palace definitely was a place of secrets. Glory could feel them hiding in the corners, ghostly but real. She sped back to the kitchen with the onions. Mrs Blossom barely looked up from her work.

'Peel 'em and slice 'em thinly. Where is that dratted boy? I sent him to find Elda, now they've both vanished.'

Glory set to, working steadily. She liked the kitchen; she felt at home here.

'Good girl. I don't know where them others is, so you're in charge of the soup.' Mrs Blossom returned to her pudding.

'Oh my Lawd!' Mrs Blossom bellowed. Rolf and Elda stood in the doorway. Elda's face was swollen as round as a cheese.

'She's been stung by a bee. I pulled out the sting, but her throat is swelling and she can't breathe properly. What shall we do?' Rolf asked, terrified.

'Take her to Miss Oleander. She'll know. Oh dear, she do look ill. Glory, stay here and make that soup, like I told you.'

The Reader

⟩ No time to read today. Dad's coming home tonight. He wasn't due 'til next week, but the job finished sooner than expected. We just got the news. I'm making him one of my Deluxe Collage Creations. I've glued a photo of his face above a skateboarder's body and written Welcome Home in cloud letters. We'll pick him up from the airport and go straight out for dinner. Mum's booked our usual table at Bombay Heaven. My parents will order palak paneer, butter chicken, lamb rogan josh and garlic naan. They'll drink bubbles and get a bit silly. I'll drink a mango lassi and get sleepy from having such a full tummy. All good.

THE WRITER

The writer strolls around her neighbour-
hood, trying to think sensibly about plot.
As she walks, she notices religious people
going door-to-door. The writer thinks it's
unreasonable. What if she began knocking
on people's doors, saying, 'Hello, would you
like to believe what I believe?' Perhaps she
could put a wandering minstrel in her book,
though. That would be good. She files it
away in a compartment in her brain marked
Possible Good Ideas For My Book. Her mind
then turns to other important matters, such
as whether it's possible to remove her profile
from Facebook, and how to stop bits of mango
lodging between her teeth. Then she reminds
herself that being a writer means you are
actually supposed to write, so she goes back
to her computer and cracks into it once more.

A CHAPTER
WITH VOMIT
IN IT

MIRABELLA WOKE SLOWLY, wriggling her toes, luxurious in her private world. Her silk sheets were embroidered with the royal crest, and soft, canopied, satin curtains draped the elaborately carved four-poster bed. Mirabella rang her silver bell loudly, but no one came. It was odd, because today was the day that her chambermaid returned to service. The princess was secretly glad that she'd have some company besides Oak and the blasted, blithering peacocks. Perhaps this time the girl would manage to hold a civil tongue, and together they could choose a suitable outfit for the ball. There was only a week to go now, each night edging her nearer the cattle market. The king and queen's instructions were clear: on the night of the ball, their daughter must choose a husband from the array of princes and noblemen who would be gathered there. Once a husband had been chosen, a wedding would shortly follow. Marriage was a terrifying thought. The constraints and constrictions of royal life were but a gilded prison, and her world already seemed lonely, boring, and restricted. Wedded life would be even more so.

Impatiently, the princess rang the bell once more, but still no one came. She deliberated for a while. There was nothing for it but to get up and face the day. At least the king was coming home, and the princess was keen to see what gift he had for her. His return had been delayed because a horse towing the royal carriage had dropped dead. Although another horse was put in its place, it took fright and reared, and the carriage ended up on its side lying in the mud. The queen was a mess of worry and complaint, as usual. She fussed mightily when the king was gone, yet fussed mightily upon his return. *She's never happy, that woman*, Mirabella reflected, then her thoughts turned to Arlo. *He's been odd, of late. He seems to be hovering. If it wasn't such a preposterous notion, I would think he admired me. However, he must know that a princess could never marry a servant.*

In the apothecary's infirmary, two girls lay side by side in narrow iron beds. Elda's face was still red and swollen, but the worst was over. Miss Oleander had administered drops of a bitter tincture, wrapped Elda's throat in cool cloths, and rubbed her limbs thoroughly throughout the long night, so the blood could flow freely, draining the poison from the dangerous area of the head and throat. Elda lay with her eyes closed and the linen bedcover pulled over her head, so as not to have to see or hear Glory's violent retching into the pail beside her. Rolf waited, anxious and patient, outside the door, but Miss Oleander would not let him in until Glory was able to sit up and drink a tisane of camomile and peppermint.

The Reader

》 What has happened? I know Elda was stung by a bee, but why is Glory sick?

THE WRITER

When she's finished worrying about her social life, her hair, heart attacks, brain tumours and climate change, the writer resumes worrying about what will happen next in her fairy story. She wants to make her characters more eccentric, their world more juicy. She considers the merits of putting a severed finger in her story, a half-crazed woman in an attic, a mentally unstable rabbit...

CHAPTER 74

IRABELLA WAS MOST dismayed by the news about Glory. Arlo, who adored gossip, waltzed in before too long, bearing a breakfast tray, and recounted what had happened.

'Imagine! She mistook things, and made a soup using daffodil bulbs instead of onions, and managed to poison herself.'

'It's a wonder she didn't poison the entire household.'

'Indeed,' said Arlo. 'She was alone in the kitchen, for Elda was stung by a bee and Mrs Blossom had rushed her to the apothecary. After making the soup, instead of sampling a spoonful, Glory ate a huge bowl of it. Apparently it tasted delicious, due to all the cream and nutmeg.'

'This palace seems jinxed with misfortune. My maid dies, Father's horse dies, then my next maid takes ill, and now I must choose my outfit for the ball myself.'

'I could help, if you like?' Arlo offered.

'I don't think that would be appropriate,' snapped Mirabella. Once Arlo had left, slightly sulkily, the princess returned to her distasteful task. It took forever to get the stupid gowns out of their boxes and silk wrappings, and none of them was the least bit suitable. In the peach satin she resembled a piglet. The orange taffeta cast her complexion as sallow as a mud puddle. The blue sprigged silk was ridiculous; the dress of a child. There was a horrid, dark stain on the ivory lace gown, and she no longer fitted the silvery-grey moire, which was a pity for it had always been her favourite. The queen was absolutely no help.

'Call in the dressmaker, if you must, Mirabella, and be fitted for a new gown,' she said. 'It will be a dash, but there may be time. Or look in my own chamber, in case there's anything suitable... You should have sorted it out earlier, and I'm most vexed about it, but right now I must lie down. I have the most dreadful headache. I'm bilious, and my eyes can't stand the light. Arlo has gone to Miss Oleander for some willow bark and poppy-head tea, and I shall rest in my chamber until your dear father arrives.'

When her mother had left, Mirabella sat alone in the gloom. How had she become this pathetic creature: the unhappiest princess in the whole wide world? She didn't wish to be so sad and sour. She didn't want to end up like her aunt, Agatha the Mad. As a young woman, Agatha was very beautiful, but when her son, Prince Oscar, died, she became ugly with grief. She ordered all mirrors to be turned to the wall and all her curtains to be drawn. Agatha insisted she possessed magic powers, though no one believed her. She spent her time alone in the dark, a pitiful crone in gowns of ragged silk and velvet, occasionally summoning an ageing count or earl to join her for tea in her musty room. As her mind became more tattered, she terrified the servants with mad mumblings about curses. She became stranger and stranger in her ways, such as having her dead dogs stuffed and adorned with jewels, to use as cushions.

'Please save me from such a pitiful fate. How can I find a happy life, locked in, as I am, to the tired ways of royalty?' Mirabella spoke out loud, then grimaced at the irony. 'Already I'm talking to myself, which is a bad sign.'

THE WRITER

The writer wonders if anyone will ever read this thing, and who they will be. If only creativity weren't so random. Sometimes it flows like a river, sometimes it tumbles like a fountain, then for no apparent reason it dries up to the odd drip from a broken tap. Broken tap days are hard. She wanders around a park, eats a very rich Florentine she's been saving for such an occasion, draws a picture in seven shades of blue. Then she begins to write.

The Reader

⟫ My father came home with his hair cut really short and a tattoo of a tiger on his shoulder. Seriously. He got the tatt in Hong Kong, on his way home. He then behaved even more out of character by ordering different dishes at dinner. Prawn Kashmiri and potato aloo, and paratha. Change is good, he explained. He said he was thinking of getting a sports car. Mum told him to get a grip.

'A motor bike?'

'No way. If you have to buy anything, make it a new wheelbarrow, and do some gardening. Cheapest cure for a midlife crisis.'

'Good plan,' Dad said. He knows when he's beaten. I don't know how he puts up with her, frankly. God, my skin is terrible. I look in the mirror and despair. My spots are multiplying. Soon I'll have to go out wearing a paper bag over my head, with holes cut for my eyes. I'm glad there are solitary things I can do, like reading. I just had an alarming thought: what if the writer died in the middle of writing a really gripping story, and you could never find out what happened next?

A FLOWERY
CHAPTER

ISS OLEANDER TOOK the wildflowers Rolf
offered and arranged them in a blue glass bottle.
'Ah, yarrow. A splendid medicinal plant.
The yellow is pretty with these blue cornflowers,
another plant with healing properties. You must
realise, Young Man, that Glory and Elda are still both
very weak. You may visit for a short while, but you
mustn't over-excite them.' The apothecary smiled at
Rolf, who was feeling particularly skinny and anxious,
and not in the least bit capable of over-exciting anyone
or anything. She went back to grinding something
smelly with her marble mortar and pestle. Now that
Rolf had been allowed into the infirmary and was
perched uneasily on a stool between the two cots, he
was flooded with shyness. He wanted to tell Glory

how glad he was she didn't die, and how winsome she looked in her white nightgown with her wild crimson hair all tumbling down, but instead a question came blurting out.

'What's yarrow used for, Miss Oleander?'

'Every part of it has a medicinal use: stems, leaves, roots and flower heads. It cures cramps and fevers, boils and bleeding, ulcers and toothaches, and purifies the blood.'

'What about cornflowers?' asked Glory, who was also feeling shy.

'The petals are brewed into an astringent tonic that soothes infections and swelling of the eyes. And now I have things to attend to.' The apothecary returned to her work at a bench on the other side of the room. To fill the clumsy silence that followed, Rolf stumbled onto the topic of the various types of bees and wasps, but Elda didn't warm to this discussion. To his relief, Glory came to the rescue.

'Rolf, when you spoke of this castle having secrets, what did you mean?'

'Well, there's definitely something mysterious about Prince Oscar and the way he died. No one will speak of it. Not even Mrs Blossom or Arlo, who usually have plenty to say about everything. All I know is that his mother, Agatha, went barking mad after his death.'

'Rolf's right,' added Elda. 'Cherry hinted of some-thing strange about Prince Oscar's death, but she wouldn't tell me the details, no matter how hard I begged.'

'Why do you ask?' Rolf enquired.

'I've found something odd, and it's troubling me.'

Elda and Rolf were fascinated to hear about Glory's discovery of the book with the empty secret compartment.

'I'll show it to you, when I am well,' she told her friends. 'Oh look, Arabella is snuffling outside the door. May she come in?'

Miss Oleander shook her head. 'Animals are not allowed inside my rooms.'

'Please,' begged Glory.

'Well, perhaps you might play with her outside for a short while. Then Rolf must return the dog to the queen's quarters.' She handed Glory a robe. Elda drifted back to sleep, and Rolf and Glory spent a most agreeable time playing with the frisky pup.

The next day, Miss Oleander allowed the two girls to leave the infirmary, having given them sensible instructions: 'Avail yourselves of rest and sunshine, and take these tinctures. Three drops in water, twice a day. And you must each come to see me, before you return to work. I will make sure you are fully recovered.'

She handed each girl a vial with their name written on it in tiny, elegant script. Glory and Elda went back to their room but could think of nothing to do in it except sleep, so they visited the kitchen, which was a big mistake. Mrs Blossom had a faint smell of brandy about her, and her mood was troubled.

'All my girls is gone. How in Lands End am I supposed to manage? Rolf is mooching around like a dementdiddly rabbit, and my cooking's going wrong at every turn. I curdled the custard today and then I burnt it, what I have never done in my entire life. Shame and woe, shame and woe . . .'

'Don't worry, Mrs B, I'll be back tomorrow,' offered Elda.

'Would you like us to help you now?' Glory asked.

'I suppose you could lend Rolf a hand. He's in the kitchen garden, picking blackberries. I need as many as you can find, for my pies.'

Rolf hadn't picked many blackberries, yet. He'd been watching a dragonfly that had landed nearby. Rolf loved the last golden days of summer, except that, because of the pies, Mrs Blossom tended to be cranky. Pastry was too fiddly for Mrs B, though she would never admit it. The kitchen was always difficult on pie days, but today was worse than usual because of all that had happened lately — and also the brandy. Rolf was glad he'd been sent to the garden. The fruit was ripe and plentiful, so it would be an easy task once he got started. When the dragonfly departed, Rolf began thinking about Glory. He'd never met a girl like Glory

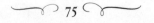

before, with her wild red hair and her innocent manner. Rolf had always been fascinated by the mysteries of the insect world, but it was new to him to be fascinated by a lovely girl. He was woken from his reverie by the arrival of Elda and Glory, and the three friends soon filled the elm-wood trug with juicy berries.

'Let's go to the library, before we take these to the kitchen,' Elda suggested. 'I want to see that secret box.'

Glory looked doubtful. Rolf grinned. 'Mrs B won't notice if we're gone a few more minutes.'

They sneaked along the corridors, narrowly avoiding the head footman who was carrying a huge floral arrangement to the entrance hall.

The library was empty. Glory went straight to the top shelf and picked up the book with the secret compartment. It was still too light.

'Here!' She held it open to her friends.

'You said there were nothing in it.' Elda sounded quite put out.

'There isn't.' Glory looked down, puzzled. 'That wasn't there last time.'

'Are you sure?' Rolf asked.

'Of course I'm sure.' Glory rubbed the torn scrap of soft coral silk between her fingers. There were tiny pearls embroidered on it.

'Let me see!' Elda grabbed the fragment. 'I seen that cloth before.'

'What? Where?'

'There was a dress made of it. I saw it, when me and Cherry was sent to help Madame Star, the dressmaker, oh, it were a year ago or more. The hours were long, and I sat all day hemming tiny stitches until my eyes were gritty, my head pulsed with pain, and my wrist ached. It were dreadful.'

'Forget about dreadful, what about the dress?'

'Don't be hurrying me, Rolf. I was just about to tell you. Cherry's job was to sort through trunks from the attic, to see what could be mended. Most of it were old soldiers' uniforms, only good for buttons and rags, but one trunk contained shawls and gowns. I remember that dress in particular, because of the unusual colour of the cloth, and them tiny pearls. Cherry was worried she'd have to cut them off, which would have been a painstaking task, but Madame Star sent the dress to the laundry to be hand-washed. She said it were a pretty gown and shouldn't be wasted.'

'I wonder where the dress is now.'

'Mrs Blossom will be wondering the same about us,' Rolf said.

Glory put the book back, tucked the morsel of fabric into her pocket, and returned to the kitchen with the others.

'Here's your blackberries, Mrs Blossom.'

'Bugger the blackberries.' The cook had her stockinged feet up on the table. Beside her sat an empty tumbler. 'I ain't making no pies. I can't be bleedin'

bothered.' With that, her head slumped on the table, and she began to snore.

Glory was gobsmacked.

'Don't worry, she does this every now and then,' explained Elda. 'She'll be right again tomorrow.'

'The royal dinner will still have to be made, though, for the king rides home tonight.' Rolf thought for a moment. 'For pudding, blackberries served in silver bowls with clotted cream.'

'What about the first course?' Glory couldn't believe that Mrs Blossom was so incapacitated or that Rolf was so readily able to take charge. What a handy, likeable person he was.

'There's a cured ham in the pantry. With new potatoes and salads fresh from the garden, it will have to do.'

'What about the servants' meals? The horsemen will be hungry,' Elda worried.

'Let's search the pantry. Bread and cheese, pickled onions, apples and figs, and a pint of ale; there's sure to be something we can serve. No one will go hungry in the palace tonight.'

The Reader

❯ It's good having Dad home. Mum is over-excitable, but he hugs her anyway. They're happy. He bought me a bracelet made of old typewriter keys, and some maple syrup lollies in the shape of little leaves. Great gifts, but it doesn't make up for the horrors of my school day. Dylan called me Pizza Face. In maths. Loud enough so that everyone could hear. Then I lost my bus pass, so my mood's not great, despite Daddo being here. When I got home, Mum and Dad had gone to buy a new sofa. In a surge of meaningless comfort eating, I scoffed two chocolate brownies from a Tupperware thingy on the bench, then when Mum got back she went ape because they were for her Stitch and Bitch group—which is nuts, because they're all on diets half the time anyway. Plus, usually she puts ridiculous signs on food I'm not allowed to eat. I went to my bedroom to escape, but Mum came straight up and knocked on the door. 'What's wrong, Darling?' I could kill her. After I kill Dylan. They can only put me in jail once, right?

THE WRITER

The writer is stuck for ideas so she asks her witty teenage nephew for help.

'What's something quirky that the king in my fairytale could do when he leaves the palace? I'm after something a bit Douglas Adams here...'

They're sitting in the King Street café, waiting for their hot drinks to arrive. Her nephew has a bit of a think.

'Have a soy latte?' he suggests, and they both crack up. But then the writer becomes excited. His idea sends her off into a whole new direction.

A CHAPTER WITH
A KING IN IT

T HE KING CAME home. Reluctantly. He'd never really wanted to be king. Being a prince was okay. You got everything you wanted — the best suits and the finest cars — plus people had to be nice to you. It was kind of like being a rock star. King Jarvis, for that was his name, was born to royalty, but he'd long ago ceased appreciating it. Fancy food tasted ordinary to him; he'd have been just as happy with a burger and fries. His marriage had been arranged, so he dutifully wed Lara, a gorgeous princess of a girl whose parents had made a shit-load of money in real estate. Unfortunately, as time went by, the king found marriage a bit of a rip-off. Lara's moods were erratic, and their only child turned out to be as grumpy as her mother. So King Jarvis found as many reasons as he could to leave the palace: snowboarding, snorkelling in Fiji, drinking soy latte in cafes with his gay chum,

Duke Eddie. Today, as he rode towards the palace, the king felt little joy. Queen Lara would greet him with a whining *Where have you been?* Then his daughter would demand *What did you bring me?* Usually, the king returned with something classy, such as a designer handbag or a new cover for Mirabella's mobile phone, but this time he had a different answer to his daughter's question.

'Nothing.'

'Crap! Parents!' muttered Mirabella. 'Why were they ever invented?'

THE WRITER

On second thoughts, perhaps not.

THE WRITER

Once upon a time, the writer had snazzy-coloured hair, but she quit colouring. She's limiting her chemical input and avoiding a tacky grow-out line, but now her hair's salt-and-pepper, which is a teensy-weensy bit ageing. The writer seeks a creative solution and settles for a red headband that looks good, in a gypsy sort of a way, and some new perfume.

The Reader

⟩ Life is dull. I felt like doing something different to my hair, so I did. It's now short and red. 'Nice,' says my father. I love Dad. He always supports and encourages me. But Mum can be a different story. 'I wish you'd asked me. I hope you know what you're doing, Nova,' she says when she sees it. Actually, I don't know what I'm doing. I'm only fifteen, and there's no map for it.

A CHAPTER WITH
A KING IN IT

THE KING CAME home. Reluctantly. He'd never wanted to be king. Being a prince was most satisfactory. You got everything you wanted — the best velvet breeches and the finest horse — and, what's more, people had to be nice to you. Being a king was not so good. Harold, for that was his name, was born to royalty and he accepted it, but he did not love it. For one thing, he'd long ago ceased appreciating the merits of his elevated position in society. The finest dishes tasted ordinary to him, the buttons on his elegant jackets still popped off at annoying moments, his horse didn't always seem to like him. Harold married the daughter of the neighbouring king and, though it was an arranged marriage, he'd accepted it willingly, for Petronilla's smile was as radiant as a sunset and her lips were red as rubies in the snow. Unfortunately, as time went by, Harold found life with his lovely bride a little harder than he'd anticipated. Some days she was sweetness and light, but sometimes she was like an angry scarecrow dancing in the wind. Harold was further saddened by the fact that, in sixteen years, he and the queen had not managed to produce a son and heir. He loved his daughter Mirabella, but she seemed so unhappy these days. She had always been a challenging child, and now she was as stormy as her mother. So, King Harold found as many reasons as he could to leave the palace. Any excuse would do: visiting the silver mines, seeking lost bears, playing chess with Tarquin, the duke of a neighbouring kingdom.

As he rode towards the palace, the king felt little joy. He knew how Petronilla would greet him. *Why didn't you come home earlier?* He could hear her demanding voice already and knew that whatever he answered would be wrong. He also knew what his daughter's greeting would be. *What did you bring me?* It had oft been his habit to return with costly baubles for Mirabella, such as a rosebud made of gold, or a dainty purse embroidered with butterflies. This time, he gave a different answer to his daughter's question. *Nothing.*

As expected, Princess Mirabella was not thrilled with her father's lack of a gift. At first she imagined that the king was playing a little trick on her and had some precious offering hidden in his pocket; a bracelet, perhaps, that she could wear to the ball.

'Where is it? Is it perchance in the inner pocket of your waistcoat? Oh, do tell.'

'I've already told you. I have no sparkling gee-gaw for you today.'

'But why, Papa? I love the gifts you bring me.'

'Are you not pleased to see me, Daughter? Is my homecoming not gift enough?' At that, the princess was silent.

'What a meal,' continued the king, wiping a drip of ale from his beard with a fine linen napkin. 'A simple meal, but a delicious one. These berries are particularly sweet.'

'Mrs Blossom is *indisposed* again. Rolf, the kitchen boy, prepared this food.' The queen had almost forgotten how annoying her husband could be, with his endlessly cheerful nature.

'Well and good, well and good. So, what other news since I've been gone?'

The queen, who'd been waiting for this very invitation, recounted the events of the preceding days: the death of Cherry, the loss of Alice, the saga of the poisoned soup, Elda's bee sting, and the lack of a suitable dress for Princess Mirabella to wear at the ball.

'A good night's sleep, My Dear, will solve most problems,' the king replied when the queen finally drew breath. He belched merrily, said he was tired, and trundled off to bed.

'Oh, the bothersome man.' The queen tossed her napkin down with irritation.

'I agree, Mama.'

Annoyingly, Petronilla then changed her mind. 'You mustn't speak ill of your dear papa, Mirabella. Perhaps he's right, and it will all seem better in the morning. I'll see you at breakfast. I've had a new thought about your dress.'

'Tell me now, Mama. I must know!'

'No, it must wait 'til the morrow. I'm exhausted, and you need your beauty sleep. You must look your best for the ball. Once you have decided on a husband, you must be sure the young man finds you as lovely as a flower.'

THE WRITER

The writer is practising Random Acts of Strange these days. Today she wiped a wet knife dry on her kitchen curtain, which—even for her—is a bit odd. She's also taken to talking to household objects, as in: 'Oh Hello, My Glasses,' and eating breakfast foods (like porridge with soy milk and raisins) for dinner. Some days, the real world does not seem as real as the world in her book.

The Reader

》 Today I found a small rubber snake under my desk at school. On the way home I cunningly placed it on a leafy branch by the wall outside the library. It looked very realistic. I also wrote the words 'Chocolate Stardust' on a scrap of paper, and tucked it in my dad's fishing hat. I think I've found my true calling. My new slogan is: Co-operate with Destiny.

CHAPTER WITH BALL GOWN AND TUMBLES

T HE MORNING DAWNED, bright and sunny. Glory ate her creamy porridge in the kitchen, where Mrs Blossom was back on her feet as if nothing had happened. Glory didn't linger, because Mrs B was busily preparing hares for a casserole, and they were hanging rather disgustingly with their heads upside down in buckets to catch the blood. She strolled across the mossy courtyard and peeped in the leadlight window of the apothecary. She wanted permission to return to service, but Miss Oleander was nowhere to be seen, so Glory retraced her steps and headed towards the main house. The courtyard bustled with life. Groomsmen tended their horses in the sunlight, dogs barked, and a noisy delivery of live ducks poked their inquisitive heads out from a large wicker basket. And there was

Arlo, chasing Arabella. Glory wished she'd time to stop and play with the merry bundle of fluff. She entered the palace by the servants' doorway, stepping over a maid who was busily scrubbing the steps. The halls were bustling, too, with hot water being transported hither and thither in huge urns, flowers being arranged, and a jester practising his juggling in the music room. When Glory arrived, the door of Princess Mirabella's chamber was open. She entered quietly and curtsied. Mirabella, who had been sitting staring glumly in the mirror, rose to greet her.

'You're back.'

Glory stared at Princess Mirabella, who quickly spoke again. 'I mean . . . good morning, are you recovered?'

'Good morning. Yes, I'm much improved, thank you.' Glory smiled. She wasn't certain what she'd do if Princess Mirabella kept behaving like a right royal pain, but they'd agreed to a fresh start so it had seemed worth risking a glare to remind the princess of it. 'What would you like me to do?'

'I must choose my outfit for the ball. Nothing I have is suitable, so we'll visit my mother's chamber. She has set aside some gowns for my consideration.'

Mirabella set off, with Glory following a few paces behind. In the queen's chamber they were met by Arlo, admiring himself in the full-length mirror. When he saw them he pretended to be wiping a smudge off the glass.

Glory had never known such a sumptuous room.

90

There were gilded mirrors, a huge carved bed hung with damask draperies, antiquities and dainty ornaments, sparkling crystal chandeliers, and an abundance of roses bathing the air with a deep, sweet fragrance.

'Good morning, Your Royal Highness.' Arlo bowed low. He was a fetching sight in blue velvet breeches, a dark green coat, and wedge-toed shoes adorned with pearl buttons. 'The queen is meeting with the head florist, but she's instructed me to help you fetch the gowns, if you wish.'

Mirabella was surprised to realise that she had begun to enjoy having Arlo around. Despite his swagger, he was very easy on the eye.

'Thank you. Please help Glory bring out the gowns.'

Glory and Arlo went into the dressing chamber, a dark exotic cavern fragrant with sandalwood and oriental perfumes. She hardly knew where to cast her gaze in the treasure trove of shoes, necklaces, jewel boxes, hat boxes, and rows of gowns in velvets, silks, and satins.

'These are the ones the queen suggests,' said Arlo, taking an armful from the end of a rack and instructing Glory to carry the others.

'Thank you, Arlo. You may go.' Mirabella amazed all three of them by giving her page a winning smile. After he'd left, she stripped down to her lace undergarments, donned a pair of white satin dancing slippers, and began trying on her mother's gowns. True to form, the princess was not readily pleased. The first gown was too frilly, the second too drab, the third too shiny. Luckily, the fourth garment found favour, much to Glory's relief, and Mirabella slipped it on.

'My mother wore this to the summer ball several years ago. I doubt anyone will remember it. What do you think?' Mirabella twirled around. It was a dreamy creation, cut from the finest silk in a delicate shade of palest green, with a plunging neckline and a swirling skirt just made for dancing.

'I like it too. You look...' Glory was searching for the right compliment when the princess twirled once more, caught her foot in the rug, tumbled into a lampshade, and landed on her royal posterior. To Glory's surprise, Mirabella remained sprawled on the carpet and started yelling.

'Stupid dress, stupid ball, stupid life! I don't want to be married off to some idiot prince!'

Glory wasn't sure what a chambermaid was meant to do in such a circumstance, but it seemed that a mixture of sympathy and sensibleness was required.

'*Must* you go to the ball?'

'Yes, you numbskull!' wailed Mirabella. 'There's no escape. It's all arranged. I'm to choose a husband.'

Glory decided to let the numbskull bit go. 'Well, if you don't *want* a husband, you could wear something quite unflattering.'

Mirabella stared at her in horror. Neither looking

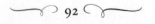

dreadful nor being forced to marry were acceptable options for this pampered princess.

'However, if you want to look beautiful, this dress is most fetching,' Glory hastened to add. 'You simply caught your foot in the hem because it's a fraction too long. Couldn't the royal dressmaker take it up for you?'

'I suppose so,' snivelled the princess.

'Perhaps you'd care to rest awhile after your tumble. Let me help you remove the gown, and while you take some ease I shall arrange to have it altered. Would you like me to bring you some hot milk with honey?'

'Yes, thank you. That would be lovely.'

Glory delivered a mug of hot milk and honey to Mirabella, collected the dress, and was given directions to the dressmaker's studio, a spacious, well-lit room looking over the rose garden. Madame Star, the dressmaker, was a tiny woman, dressed entirely in lemon yellow, who was sewing what looked like an extremely large curtain. Glory wondered why many of the inhabitants of the palace were an odd size: the queen so tall, Elda so runty, Mrs Blossom so huge, and now this small person. Although, she had to admit that Rolf and Arlo both seemed to be just perfectly proportioned.

'May I help you?'

'I'm Glory, Princess Mirabella's new maid. I've brought the princess's gown. It needs the hem altered, so she can wear it to the ball.'

Madame Star gave Glory a strange look, but her words seemed normal enough.

'How much should it be taken up?'

'About this much.' Glory indicated with finger and thumb, having not thought to measure.

'I'll tack it up, then you can take it back to the princess for her to try.' Madame Star took a pin from her sleeve, made the necessary mark on the hem, and set to work. 'Would you care to look around?'

'Yes, please.' Glory was entranced by the wide array of fabrics, some neatly folded, some in large rolls: crepe, chambray, georgette, lawn, mousseline, organza, taffeta, and tulle. There were cottons, yarn and ribbons in every shade, and filmy wisps of chiffon drifted from a dressmaker's dummy like angels' scarves. A vase of red peonies dropped fat petals beside a workbook displaying sketches of unusual border patterns. Glory was about to comment on the intricate designs when she felt a big sneeze coming. Without thinking, she reached into her pocket, but instead of a handkerchief she pulled out the scrap of fabric she'd found in the secret box.

'Where did you get that?' Madame Star's voice was sharp and serious.

Glory explained how she'd come to be in possession of the little piece of coral silk. 'First the box was empty, but then this appeared in it. It's as if...'

'Yes?' the dressmaker asked quietly.

'As if someone's trying to tell me something, but what?'

'Come sit with me, Child. There are things you must know, and the time has come for you to hear them.'

'Shouldn't I be getting back? Mirabella may need me.' Though she could not explain why, Glory was flooded with sudden, dark fear. An age-old, ominous cloud of doom penetrated her heart, her stomach, her very bones. It made no sense, but she wanted nothing more than to run for her life.

'Don't worry. It won't hurt that girl to wait.' Madame Star smiled and winked, and the atmosphere lightened a little.

'The story I'm about to tell you is a sad one. But you must be brave and open your heart and mind to what I'm about to say. Do you have the courage?'

'I think so.'

'The cloth is a scrap of the dress your mother was wearing the day Prince Oscar died. I imagine it was put there by Miss Oleander, to lead you to me.'

'Why couldn't Miss Oleander tell me herself, if there is something to be told?' Glory felt great confusion.

'Listen carefully and you will understand. When Rosamund, your mother, came to the palace, she and Persia, or Miss Oleander as she is known now, became best friends. They were like two white roses in the moonlight, radiant and fresh. Their lightness and laughter attracted Prince Oscar, despite Persia and

Rosamund's lowly rank. The three young people loved to spend time together, walking in the gardens or sitting by the river. Their liaison was much frowned upon, but the young prince did not care. As time went on, your mother and the prince fell in love, for Cupid's bow cares nothing for convention. At that time, Persia was apprenticed to the old apothecary, training in herbs and arcane rituals, and that is how she acquired the book.'

'What book is that?' Glory wondered what all this had to do with her. Remembering her weary mother, cooking gruel and mending, she struggled to understand how this tale could possibly be true.

'It was a grimoire, a book of spells. Persia was born into a family of healers, and she had magic powers, though not yet strong ones. Your mother, being the seventh daughter of a seventh daughter, also had mystical abilities, but again her powers were undeveloped, unruly, like breezes not yet tamed. The two young women wove a spell to enable Oscar and Rosamund to spend one perfect day together, outside time, before the prince was betrothed to someone else. Rosamund would never be queen, yet surely she deserved one sweet day of happiness. They cast the spell light-heartedly, not fully believing it would work. On a summer's morning, Persia braided your mother's long golden hair with ribbons and dressed her in a borrowed gown of coral silk. Your mother went alone to the meadow to await the prince.'

'Did they get their perfect day?'

'Tragically, on his way to meet his love, Prince Oscar fell from his horse and was killed. A terrified servant boy, who'd overheard the plan, let the secret out. Oscar's mother, Agatha, was crazed with grief. That's when she cast a curse.'

'Why are *you* telling me this? Why didn't my mother or Miss Oleander tell me?'

'Those associated with a curse are forbidden to speak of it, but I am not. I've been waiting for you to come. It was only a matter of time until this unfolding of events.'

'Does everyone around here have magic powers?' Glory mumbled.

'Not everyone, but Agatha certainly did, though many did not believe in her abilities. Her magic was strong. Furious and bitter, she took revenge, believing that your mother had caused Oscar's death.'

Glory's heart trembled. She'd forgotten all about Mirabella, all about her duties. Her body was cold as marble. An ill wind whistled down the edges of time. She waited. 'What was the curse?'

'Sit down, My Dear,' Madame Star said gently. She took Glory's arm and led her to the velvet couch. 'Would you care for some elderflower cordial?'

'What?' Glory was in a state of shock. Nothing made sense. 'No, thank you,' she managed to murmur. 'I want to hear what happened. Please, I must know.'

Madame Star knew there was no sense in delaying any further.

'In return for the loss of her son, Agatha demanded that Rosamund's firstborn child, whether male or female, be sent to the palace. This would happen when the child turned fifteen, the same age Prince Oscar was when he died.'

'But...' Glory was still confused. 'To leave my mother and live in the palace...surely that is not so bad?'

Madame Star looked down at her hands. There was no way to avoid the news she must deliver.

'The curse also declared that, at the palace, a fatal accident would befall Rosamund's child.'

Glory, white-faced, said nothing, for what was the use? It seemed there was no way to escape whatever lay in store.

'However,' Madame Star continued. 'What...stop! You have not heard...'

But it was too late, for Glory had leapt to her feet and bolted.

THE WRITER

She packs her red suitcase and flies home
to her own bed, garden, kitchen, life. Joy!
The writer's editor has seen the first part
of her manuscript and says the fairytale is
going well, and she has noted her helpful
suggestions in the margins, for the writer
to take or leave. The writer thinks long
and hard about the tiny pencilled notes. She
wishes she could <u>find</u> the problems instead
of having to fix them. She goes back to
worrying... Why did she ever put a curse in
there? Should Mirabella and Glory become
friends? Will Mirabella marry? Maybe she's
gay? Maybe she runs away? With Arlo? Maybe
she dies? Maybe she tricks a prince into...

In an effort to avoid these conundrums,
the writer sets off to perform her daily
errands: post office, library, groceries. On
the street outside the library foyer, she
treads on some sticky chewing gum, which
takes ages to get off her shoe. Bugger.

The Reader

⟩ It began with roasted vegetables and ended with...
well, you'll see. Last night we had chicken salad
and roasted veggies for dinner: pumpkin, onions,
potatoes, and a whole head of garlic—an idea Mum
got from a cooking show. We squeezed the creamy,
soft garlic onto Turkish bread. Delicious. However,
in the car this morning, Mum said I reeked of garlic.
I'm already pretty low down on the popularity stakes,
and I couldn't face school with another reason for
Dylan to hassle me. I panicked a bit, imagining
her calling me Stink Breath or Smelly Girl, while
Toby and Nigel laughed. Luckily, Mum remembered
there was an old packet of chuddy in the glove box,
so I went to school chewing gum, for ultra breath
freshness. During first period, in Social Studies, we
were having a discussion about the changing role of
fathers in families, and Dylan piped up, in a really
loud voice, 'Nova's father goes away a lot. I don't
blame him.' No one laughed much. In fact the room
went mortifyingly quiet. Dylan was sitting in front
of me, tossing her long shiny hair. So I stuck my

chewing gum in it; took out the sticky pink wad and rubbed it right into the strands. What satisfaction. Short-lived, though, because it was straight to the headmaster for both of us. Mr D tried to untangle Dylan's sticky, knotted hair, but it was impossible. Miss R, the deputy, was called in and suggested eucalyptus oil, but there was none to be found, so they phoned Dylan's mother and asked her to bring some in. Dylan faked a few tears, and I tried to explain what a bitch she's been. At first, Mr D couldn't get past the chewing gum incident, but finally it sank into his pea-sized brain that there were issues here beyond me being a hair-wrecking maniac. So now Dylan and I have to go to the school counsellor together, tomorrow at lunchtime.

'There are always two people in a personality clash,' Mr D announced.

Bunkum! I thought, but managed to keep my mouth shut.

I didn't want to tell Mum about what happened, but the school sent a note home. Now she's all anxious and sad. I'm feeling guilty and miserable and really worried about what tomorrow will bring. This is *so* not my fault, but if there's any way to make it seem like it is, Dylan will find it. Glory's not the only one who's cursed.

A VERY
IMPORTANT
CHAPTER

THE PRINCESS WAITED and waited, but still Glory did not return, with or without the gown. Finally, Mirabella got dressed and headed for her mother's chambers but instead met the queen in the gloomy grand hall.

'What is it, Daughter? I'm eager to give Mrs Blossom instructions for tonight's dinner. You haven't fallen out with your chambermaid already, I pray?'

'On the contrary. Glory was most civil, and I was too, Mama. We chose your green silk for the ball. Glory went to the dressmaker to have the hem altered, but that was a veritable age ago. She has vanished.'

'I doubt she has vanished. You must not be so melodramatic. It takes time to sew a tidy hem, My Dear. Accompany me to the kitchen, and we shall send someone to the dressmaker to find out what's become of her.'

The kitchen was fragrant with spices because Mrs Blossom was making her finest preserves, which were to complement the meats on the evening of the ball. Elda sat on a bucket, glumly peeling onions. She sniffed with envy when Rolf was given leave of his task.

'Off to Madame Star, Lad. There's no hurry for the gown, but the princess needs her chambermaid, so fetch Glory to the kitchen,' instructed the cook.

Rolf smirked. Removing apricot pits from ripe fruit was a messy business, and seeing Glory would be a welcome treat.

Mrs Blossom dusted her hands on her apron and fetched her leather-bound recipe book. Princess Mirabella sat quietly while the cook and the queen added several new dishes to the feast menu: wild boar cassoulet, and apricot syllabub dusted with saffron. The kitchen was such a friendly place of warmth and delectable smells. It seemed to the princess that the life of a commoner would be far more pleasant than her burdensome life of royalty. She wished she could wear a dusty apron and cook hearty fare, enjoy ordinary things, and most of all marry whom she wished. Mirabella didn't realise that Elda was cranky, or that Mrs Blossom was worried about the freshness of the day's meat. All she saw was the marmalade cat basking under the table, the cheery bunch of daisies, and the sun beaming in the window on this peaceful morning. As she pondered the joys of a simple life, the princess's idyll was interrupted by a flurry of footsteps and the sudden appearance of Madame Star and Rolf.

'Glory's run away!'

Mrs Blossom gasped. Elda jumped up, scattering onion skins everywhere, which frightened the cat, and Queen Petronilla turned very pale.

'Does she know?' Her question was directed at Madame Star.

'Yes, Your Highness, but...'

'But what?' The queen's tone was most serious.

'She only knows of the curse. She did not wait to hear anything I said after that. She just ran...'

Glory swept her skirts around her and ran — out of the studio and away from the palace. She sprinted as fast as she could, past flower gardens, past trees cut into unusual shapes, past vegetable gardens and orchards, along the willow-lined brook, and she kept running until she was deep in the woods. Exhausted, Glory threw herself down onto a mossy log under a yew tree. Her heart was pounding and her limbs felt strangely heavy, like dead tree branches. So, this was how it must be. Events of the past, dark and ill, had conspired against her, and she must die. It all made terrible sense, now. Why her mother had always seemed sad about Glory's indenture to the palace. Why the queen had made her stay in the palace instead of sending her home. She, Glory, was to give her life in exchange for the life of Prince Oscar. Although she understood the way things must be, Glory was flooded with despair. *I've done nothing to deserve this*, she thought miserably. *I'm a pawn in a twisted game. I want to grow old and be happy. I want to dance with the one I love, to marry on a spring day, to have a child and sing to it, to feed it milk and rusks. I want to breathe the sweet air of summer, see the changing colours of autumn, wrap myself in a red woollen cloak on a chill winter's day. I want life. I want my life.* Glory looked around the dark woods. It seemed that the trees spoke to her in a language she could not understand, and a vast unknowingness came upon her. She lay down on the grass and wept, and then she fell asleep.

THE WRITER

The writer has read about such things, in articles about famous writers and their work. 'My characters just started doing things by themselves. They took over the text and began behaving in ways that suited them.' But the writer has never believed it. The way it seemed to her was that being a writer was a chance to play God on paper. You created little puppet people, then you did what you wanted with them. Except that the writer had planned for Glory to remain in the room with Madame Star. After the girl heard of the curse, something else was about to be disclosed. But Glory had other ideas. Instead of waiting to hear the next bit, she took to her feet and ran away into the forest, all by herself, with no regard for the writer's plan. So now the writer must follow Glory into the dark woods...

The Reader

》 Ms Golightly only began working as a counsellor at our school this year. She sports a diamond in her nose, which is pretty cool for a teacher. She's not too old, skinny, and wears unusual outfits—sporty-grunge meets boho-indie. Today she wore black, baggy hemp pants, black sneakers, a black t-shirt with blue flowers on it, and a black headband pushing back her messy blonde hair.

'Come on in, Girls.' Dylan and I had both arrived at the appointed time. We didn't greet each other, just stood dumbly outside 'til she ushered out Max O'Connor—who's always in the shit—and called us in. Dylan and I sat at each end of the sofa, not looking at each other, and Ms G sat opposite us, in a red wicker chair. There was a box of tissues on the table and an ivory statue of an Oriental goddess on the windowsill, beside a posy of violets.

'Okay, here's the deal,' Ms Golightly said in a friendly tone. 'You've been sent here to me because of yesterday's incident with the chewing gum, and also because it seems there's some sort of problem between you. Is that right?'

We both nodded.

'This is what we're going to do. I'll toss a coin to see who goes first. You're each going to take a turn at saying what you think the problem is. Just call it as you see it. When one of you is speaking, the other listens. No butting in, no arguing. Make an effort to hear and understand. See if you can imagine what it is like to be in the other person's shoes. When you've both had a turn, we'll see what needs doing next. Okay?'

We both nodded mutely. I resisted the temptation to say I'd rather take party drugs and dance naked on the table. When I'm tense, silliness is my first resort, but it doesn't usually go down well with grown-ups. Instead I crossed my fingers behind my back and prayed that Dylan would lose the toss and have to go first. But she didn't. Ms Golightly gave me an encouraging smile, Dylan gave a smug grin, and my guts turned to concrete. I stared at the tiny goddess in the window. Maybe it was a trick of the light, but I could swear she winked at me. I remembered something we learnt in drama when we worked with masks. *Don't rehearse. Take a deep breath and go for it.*

'Dylan treats me like shit. I don't like it. I don't deserve it and I'm sick of it.' I stared at my classmate. She was stony-faced, but I noticed her swallow nervously. She couldn't hold my gaze. She glanced down at her fingers, and I saw that her nails were short and bitten. I'd never noticed that before.

'Care to give some examples of Dylan's behaviour?' Ms Golightly asked.

'Not really.' I intended to play it safe and strong, and not say much, but then more came blurting out of me. 'Okay then. She sniggers and sneers. She put a nasty sticker on my back. She hid my bag and she calls me Pizza Face. Yesterday, in front of our whole class, she insinuated that my dad chooses to work overseas because he doesn't like me. That's when I snapped and put the chuddy in her hair. I'm not sorry, by the way.'

'Thank you for sharing, Nova. Okay, Dylan, your turn.'

Silence. Dylan just kept staring down at her lap while the silence became more and more uncomfortable, for me at least. After what seemed like forever, Ms Golightly spoke in a firm but fair tone.

'This may be hard for you, Dylan, but participating today is not optional. Here's your chance to say what's on your mind. You need to take responsibility for your part in what's been going on between you and Nova. It's time to deal. Let's hear from you.'

Just when I thought the nerve-racking silence would never end, the oddest thing happened: Dylan started to cry.

CHAPTER

THURSDAY WITH

SURPRISES AND

STARBLOSSOM

WHEN GLORY WOKE it was nearing evening, and the woods were silent and eerie in the dying light. Despondently, she began to make her way back to the palace, for there was no point trying to hide. Once a curse has been cast, it can always find its victim. *I must be valiant and face what lies ahead*, she resolved, but the plucky girl's head clamoured with questions. *Shall I know the manner of my death? Will the cruel blow strike at any moment?*

Glory trudged back across the meadow. As she entered the orchard, she heard the birds singing their nightfall songs. An apricot squished beneath her soft leather shoe, releasing a pungent fruity fragrance. Though Glory had vowed to have courage, a small sob escaped her. *This is what I will miss*, she knew, with heartbreaking clarity. *I will miss the ordinary things: birdsong, evening, fruit...*

'Glory! Where have you been? Everyone's looking for you ... Thank goodness I've found you at last.'

Glory lifted her gaze, and there was her friend, peeping through the yew hedge. At the sight of dear, scruffy, worried Elda, she burst into tears, despite every intention to contain her emotions.

The two girls sat down together on a garden seat made of twisted oak. Elda patted Glory's back gently, trying to calm her sobbing friend. A little grey partridge landed nearby, as if to encourage.

'It'll be all right, I promise...'

'Elda, you don't understand. You don't know what has befallen me.' Glory's words came out sharper than she had intended it.

'But I *do* know. I were in the kitchen when Madame Star came to tell of a curse against you, and that you'd run away when you heard of it. Everyone was there, even Queen Petronilla and Princess Mirabella. Rolf is beside himself, and Mrs Blossom became hysterical, saying you'd drowned yourself in the stream.'

'Why should I drown myself? I'm to die soon enough anyway.'

'But we must hasten back!' Elda jumped to her feet.

'I see no reason to hurry.'

'There's something more you must hear...'

'What?' Glory asked wearily. 'If the dressmaker

wants to describe the manner of my death, I'm in no hurry to know the details.'

'No, it's not that,' Elda butted in anxiously. 'Madame Star were most insistent. "The poor girl does not know the entire story," she kept saying. There must be more for you to learn. Come, let's hurry back. Darkness falls, and we must let them know that you are safe.'

Safe. I think not, thought Glory bleakly but it was not poor Elda's fault. The two girls held hands and hurried between the rows of herbs, past the pansy beds, and through the perfumed rose gardens. When they reached the kitchen, Rolf greeted them with joy and amazement, and ushered them inside.

'Lawd! You are found!' Mrs Blossom's face lit up and she dabbed her eyes with a tartan kerchief. 'You are to go at once to the royal chambers. Rolf, accompany her.'

'May I go, too?' Elda asked.

'No, you stay here. We shall have some supper waiting for when they return.'

Glory and Rolf made their way up the grand stairway and through the quiet candlelit halls. Neither said a word until Rolf managed to mumble how glad he was she was found. Glory smiled wanly at him, but could not think of a fitting reply. She felt tired, so very tired, and utterly despairing.

'In you go,' said Rolf, when they arrived at the door. 'I'll be waiting here for you.'

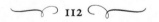

THE WRITER

The writer has been channelling her inner
librarian instead of her inner spoonchild,
eating plenty of salad but not enough cake.
She's been walking miles in comfy old track
pants, but not lounging lazily on her bed in
her kimono, reading old magazines. Lately, she
hasn't even allowed herself a teensy-weensy
bit of retail therapy. How come she keeps
forgetting the obvious? 'People of the World,
Relax!' as Kurt Vonnegut said. So, the writer
gets out her coloured pencils, her Mexican
recipe book, her sewing box and wonderful
fabrics. She paints a flowerpot turquoise,
drinks champagne on a Wednesday, buys herself some flowers, just because. The more she
smiles at her life, the more it smiles back
at her, and the more the writing flows.

The Reader

〉 'My dad's got cancer.' The words hung in the air, like unexpected visitors from outer space. Dylan had nearly stopped crying, but not quite. Ms Golightly passed the tissues, and Dylan blew her noise noisily. There was no way anyone could have predicted this. I could see even Ms G wasn't quite sure where to go next, but she took a breath and spoke quietly, kindly.

'That's awful news. Have you just found out, Dylan?'

'No. He was diagnosed a year ago. My parents want to keep it quiet, so I wasn't meant to tell anyone. He's been having all these horrible treatments . . .'

'Chemo?'

'Yeah, and radiation therapy. He had an operation, too, but they're not sure that they've got it all.'

I turned to the tiny statue. She wasn't winking now. I didn't know what to do with what I'd just heard. I felt sick in my tummy. I was really sorry for Dylan. But I was also still wondering why she'd been so ghastly to me. Ms Golightly was wondering, too, because after some more uncomfortable silence she continued.

'Of course you're devastated by your father's illness, Dylan. My heart is with you, and we can come back to this and talk more about it. But I need to hear your version of what's gone wrong between you and Nova. Are you able to talk about that for a while?'

'I guess.' Dylan sniffed. 'Nova and I have never been friends, but we're in most of the same classes. She used to hang out with Annie, the girl who went to study violin at some posh school in Sydney. Since then, Nova acts like she's better than everyone else. All the teachers adore her because she's so bright, and she knows it. She's snobby; too good to mix with us ordinary people. I guess I might have given her a bit of a hard time...' Her voice trailed off.

I still don't get why you've been such a bitch to me, I wanted to demand.

'I'd like to know how this relates to your father's illness, Dylan. There seems to be a connection there for you.'

'Yeah, well, it just really seems unfair. Her dad's got everything going for him, like good health and a glamorous job. Nova gets pressies from around the world; she flashes them around, jewellery and lollies and stuff...'

Bloody hell! Dylan's got me so wrong! It's totally unfair, the way she's twisted good stuff into bad, like me sharing my dainty candies from Japan in Social Studies. I thought that it was pretty generous of me, actually, and I don't know how she knew about the bracelet. I never boasted about it. Oh, I remember, someone commented on it in the library and Dylan must have overheard. Unbelievable. She's made it seem like I was bragging. As for thinking I'm up myself, well, up her, I say! It's not my fault her father has cancer. I'm busting to say something but I don't think I'm meant to. Ms G continues doing her thing.

'I hear it seems unfair to you that Nova appears to be happy and independent and achieving at school when you aren't feeling good about life. It also seems unjust that her dad is healthy while your father is facing a major illness. To you that kind of sucks. Right?'

Dylan grunted.

Ms Golightly smiled encouragingly, then turned to me. 'Nova, would you care to respond?'

'I'm sorry about the cancer, for real, but the rest of it is bollocks. I haven't had any friends since Annie left. I just do my schoolwork and get on with it. I'm not snobby! Dylan's the popular one. She's always surrounded by her mates, plus she's in lah-lah land about our family. My father's job isn't glamorous. He gets jetlag, and he misses planes, and he arrives home exhausted. Mum really misses him when he's away, which makes her crabby, so it isn't all sweetness and light at our house. Far from it. Last night, Mum was a mess because one of her favourite patients died. She's a receptionist at a rest home, and some of her days are very depressing. Everyone's got their troubles, and I don't think it's reasonable that I cop Dylan's shit...'

I glared at her and she stared blankly back at me. Ms G took some caramels out of her pocket and offered us one each.

'Thanks for being honest and for listening without interrupting, both of you. There's a couple of things I'd like to say. First, it's easy to displace your feelings. For example, you hate your haircut and you feel ugly, so you snap at your brother instead of sticking with your uncomfortable feelings about your hair. May I suggest that this might be what's happened for you, Dylan? You feel really shite about your dad and his illness, but it's easier to hate Nova than to stick with those awful, sad, powerless feelings. Make any sense?'

'Yeah, maybe,' Dylan replied grudgingly.

Ms Golightly got up, fetched the ivory statue, and held it out to us.

'This is a Buddhist deity called Kuan Yin. She's the goddess of compassion. It's said that she holds all our troubles in her arms, because she sees the ten thousand sufferings of humankind.'

'I don't see what that's got to do with anything.' Dylan sounded pissed off. I felt a fluttering of warmth towards her, because I'd been thinking the same thing but I hadn't had the nerve to say it.

'For me, Kuan Yin is a reminder that everyone has

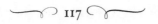

crappy stuff to deal with. There's an old Chinese saying: No house can hang out a sign saying *No Trouble Here*. We often think we're the only person struggling, but actually everyone is. We all have sorrows and joys, successes and tragedies. It makes me feel kinder and more compassionate when I remember that. Just something to think about.' Ms Golightly looked at her watch, stood up, and put the goddess statue back.

'Right, I've decided what to do. Starting now, once a week, for a month, you guys are going to spend an hour together. It's up to the pair of you to decide how to spend it. There's only one rule. You have to have fun together. Play, if you will.'

'No way! Why?' Dylan took the words out of my mouth.

'I don't suppose *Because I Said So* will do it for you?' Ms Golightly asked perkily.

'Nah.' This time we answered in unison.

'Didn't think so. Worth a shot, though. Okay, here's why. I think it will do you both good.'

'Do we have to?' I thought I'd get in first, this time.

'Yep. Come back and see me next week, same time, same place, to let me know how you get on. Okay, Ladies, that's it for today. That'll be a hundred bucks each.'

We stared at her in dismay. This was getting too weird.

'Kidding.'

CHAPTER
MOONBEAM AND
A QUARTER

'PERSIA OLEANDER'S POWERS have greatly improved since that time.'

Glory stared at the queen blankly. Nothing seemed real: the dressmaker's news, the forest, being here at night in the queen's company. Perhaps soon she would wake up and find herself safe at home with her mother, sitting by the fire, mending her brothers' socks. Glory dug her fingernails into her palm, in case it woke her from this nightmare. But no, she was here, in the royal chambers, weary and frightened, without an escape. The queen sat nearby on a velvet sofa, her little dog asleep beside her. Glory wished she had a friend like Arabella. And as she thought this, Arabella jumped down and settled herself at Glory's feet.

'Listen carefully, My Dear. This is what Madame Star was desperate to tell you this morning before you ran away. Naturally, your mother and Persia were horrified by Agatha's curse. The fatal result from her first attempt at magic left your mother unwilling to explore her potential any further. But Persia spent the next years strengthening her magical powers. She felt dreadfully responsible for what had happened. When her abilities became powerful enough, she cast a spell designed to weaken Agatha's magic. The curse could not be entirely undone, but it *has* been moderated. Are you following me?'

'Yes, Your Highness.'

'Between the moment you hear about Agatha's curse and midnight on the next full moon, you must save a life. If, before the morning light dawns after that moon, you have achieved this task, your own life will be saved. Do you understand?'

Glory's thoughts tumbled like rocks in a landslide. She swallowed.

'Not really. How will I know what to do? What if there is no life possible to save? Or what if there is a chance to save a life but I do not succeed?'

'These are questions that can't be answered in advance. The future cannot be seen, but you have been granted a chance. I trust fortune will be on your side. Right now, you are pale with shock and weariness. Is Arlo waiting to escort you? Have him take you to the kitchen for your supper, then perhaps a night in the infirmary would be the best thing. Miss Oleander can check your pulse, and may provide a sleeping draught to help you rest.'

'Not Arlo, but Rolf, the kitchen boy . . .'

'Then have him escort you to the kitchen.'

'So?' Rolf asked eagerly, when Glory appeared.

'Supper. Then I'm to sleep in the infirmary. I am weary Rolf, so very weary. But the queen was strangely kind to me, and this is what she has told me . . .'

In the warm kitchen, Mrs Blossom ladled chicken broth with dumplings into bowls, and Elda brought a beaker of warm, sweetened milk. While Glory ate, Rolf recounted the new development, at which Elda began to buzz with excitement, but Mrs Blossom, seeing Glory's exhaustion, stepped in.

'Hush, Dear. Right now the lass needs her rest.'

As Rolf and Glory approached, they saw Persia Oleander standing in the courtyard, looking up into the night sky. Tiny stars sparkled, and the waxing moon hung high above them.

'The full moon is a mere few days hence,' she said quietly to the two young people. Glory opened her mouth to reply, but didn't get a chance. 'The night of the ball. A night of great importance, as you know.

Now, come on in. Let me bathe your feet and tuck you into bed. There's nothing more to be said or done that won't wait until morning.'

Rolf squeezed Glory's hand and slipped away. Before she knew it, the weary girl was tucked under a cashmere spread, fast asleep.

After Glory left, the queen took off her too-tight shoes and put on her ermine slippers, then made her way to her husband's chamber, where the king sat reading a large map by the light of an ornate candelabra.

'Hello, My Love,' he said, scratching his beard. 'You are truly a sight for sore eyes.'

The queen felt a sudden fondness for her husband of so many years. They discussed the matter of Glory.

'As you say, it's not in our hands,' declared the king, 'but let us pray that the new magic is efficacious, and that the girl is able to save two lives: another's and thus her own.'

'Indeed.' The queen sighed deeply. 'If only that was all that troubled me...'

'You refer to the matter of our daughter and the ball, I believe?' The king spoke gently, and once more the queen's heart softened towards him. 'What is your main concern? Is it the lack of a suitable husband for Mirabella? Or is it her lack of desire for any husband at all?'

'It is both. The invitations have gone out far and

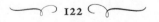

wide. Every prince within the land will be there. We couldn't have included a wider assortment of men, but many of them are so obviously flawed.'

'Clearly, Mirabella will not be interested in William the Bastard, Bernard the Mad, or Swythyn the Stupid,' agreed the king. 'However, there are others who are more suitable, surely? Prince Leonard, son of King Gilbert, is a dashing young fellow, and his older brother Timothy, though not as handsome, is a witty chap. He's gallant, and highly skilled in falconry.'

'True enough, but it's rumoured that Prince Leonard is enamoured of his distant cousin Isabella, so perhaps he will not pay Mirabella much attention.'

'Timothy, then?'

'Perhaps.' The queen sighed once more. 'Mirabella is so against the idea of marriage. I fear she will refuse to choose a husband at all, just to be difficult. And then what shall we do?'

'Come here, My Dove, lean your head on my shoulder. Worrying will not solve it. I've been poring over this map all night. Perhaps there is a goldmine somewhere, waiting to be found.'

The Reader

❯ Outside Ms G's office, Dylan and I stared at each other.

'So, we have to hang out together and play. Superb.' My irony wasn't wasted on Dylan.

'Yes, frigging lovely.'

Nigel Brown dawdled past with his shoelaces undone. He's a total turkey, that guy, but it gave us something to stare at. We stood there awkwardly.

'We'll still be here at Christmas if we don't sort something out,' Dylan offered finally.

'Fair enough. I went first with the touchy-feely stuff so you can go first with the plan.'

'I can't think of anything.' Dylan became incredibly interested in the dry skin around her fingernail. Then she made a stab at a solution. 'Okay, come over to my house after school today. I'll have thought of something by then.'

'Really?' The thought of spending time at Dylan's house was as appealing as pouring dog's urine into my ears, or eating fried shoelaces.

'Yep. Know where I live?'

'Opposite the Aquacentre, yeah?'

'You got it.'

'See you later, then.'

We walked back to class together without speaking, pretending none of it had happened.

After school, I went by the nursing home to tell Mum what was up. *I'm visiting a friend*, I scribbled on a piece of paper, because she was on the phone. Mum waved and gave me the thumbs-up. I bought a Triple Ripple ice-cream and ate it slowly, sitting on the bench outside the corner store. I couldn't think of any more delaying tactics, so I made my way to Dylan's house, a wooden villa with a cottage garden of pink roses, jasmine, and a colourful glass mosaic birdbath.

Dylan opened the door before I'd had time to knock.

'Nice birdbath,' I said, for lack of anything better.

'Yeah, my mum's into mosaics,' she replied, ushering me quickly down the hall and upstairs to her bedroom.

'Mine was, too, for a while. She's a hobby nutter. Thai cooking, Spanish For Beginners, and mosaics ... now she goes to Stitch and Bitch. They knit and sew stuff.'

'Cool,' said Dylan. At least she was trying to be friendly. Her long blonde hair was tucked under a cap, and she was wearing white shorts and a white singlet top. I realised she was a lot skinnier than she looked in school uniform. She looked a bit frail, to be honest. Interesting, 'cause she always seemed such a tough cookie. Her room was a bomb site, but it reminded me of mine, with clothes everywhere and heaps of random stuff, including a huge heart made of red glass beads. Dylan plonked herself on her unmade bed and offered me the orange beanbag.

'So, whassup?' I asked her.

'That's the problemo. I can't really think of anything to do. Want to cook something?'

'Nah, not really.' I didn't want to sound rude, so I continued. 'Last time Annie and I cooked we made hot chocolate pudding, but we forgot to put in the sugar so the result tasted and looked like soil. Annie's guinea pig wouldn't even touch it, and her mother was really pissed 'cause we wasted heaps of expensive ingredients. Plus, I ate an ice-cream on the way here, so I'm not really hungry. Cooking is best when you're hungry, I find.'

'True...how about drawing?'

'If you want to. It's not really my forte. I like doing collage, though.'

'Let's do that, then. Art and craft—it's sort of play, isn't it?'

'Reckon. Anyhow, what's the worst she can do to us?'

Dylan scrounged around in her desk and found

cardboard, stickers, pens, crayons and—after a raid downstairs—two pairs of scissors and a pile of old magazines. We sat at the desk together and started to cut.

'Watch out for the glue, it's gone all squidgy. Get this,' Dylan said, as she hacked out a picture of some handsome dude in a boy band. 'Nicole Richie's called her baby son Sparrow. Dumb name, for sure. Her daughter's called Harlow, it says here. Imagine going through life with those names!'

'Hmm,' I replied. I'm trying to decide whether to cut hearts or stars out of a floral wallpaper advertisement.

'What are the worst things to name a kid, do you think?'

'Haystack, maybe?'

'My cousin in Tasmania called her kid Salmon.'

'You're joking, right?'

'Nah, I wish. No one in the family knows what to say about it.'

'Poor kid. You know what I hate? Those really smarty-pants rich-people names, like Ophelia and Maximilian...'

'Fuchsia and Pepper...'

'Benedict and Saffron.'

'Those people are SINDs, for sure.'

'SINDs?'

'Strangely Idiotic Name Dimwits.'

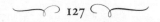

'Clearly. They should get a grip and become...
um...GINDs, Good Imaginative Name Donors.'

We kicked this game around for a bit. We decided
it was Turn Everything into an Acronym Day. Dylan
decided to be a WRITER when she grows up: a Well Read
Interesting Tinkerbelle Eating Ratatouille. I claimed
that in my last life I was one of the SHAKESPEARES: Sexy
Happy Amazing Kings Endlessly Shopping Passionately
in Extra Appealing Rainbow Energy Shoes. Then, we
moved on to creating interesting days, such as Make
Up Your Own Language Day, Find Money and Give It
Away Day, Sound Terrible But Sing Anyway Day, and
Random Chihuahuas Running Amok in the Streets Day.

'How about Be Yourself Day?' said Dylan.

'Good one. Although, who else can you possibly
be? Like in the song: *Be yourself. Everyone else is
taken.* Scary, I sound like my mother. She's always
quoting from self-help books.'

Dylan grinned. 'Yeah, we don't want it to turn
into Be Your Mother Day...'

As if on cue, Dylan's mother came pounding up
the stairs and stuck her head in the door.

'Hi, Sweetie. Oh, you've got someone here...'

'Yeah, this is Nova. Nova, meet my mum. We're
making cards.'

I'd seen Dylan's mother before, actually, outside
the school. She's fat, and wears big, loud outfits, and
has a friendly face.

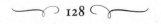

'Lovely. Hey, do you girls want some Milo or anything?'

'No, I'm fine, thanks.' I glanced at the clock by the bed. 'Actually, I didn't realise it was after six. I should get going. My mother will be expecting me.'

'Nice cards.' Dylan's mum came over to look closer. Mine was mainly hearts, and Dylan's was mainly guys.

'Looks like a bit of a love theme going on here, Girls.'

'Get outta here,' Dylan said, embarrassed.

I felt awkward, too. I took my card and headed for the door. 'Okay, gotta bounce. See you at school, then?'

'Yeah, *ciao*.'

Dylan followed me downstairs to see me out. I was back on the street. It was a warm evening. I couldn't believe I'd had an almost-good time.

THE WRITER

The writer is sad. The world contains so much tragedy: tsunami in Samoa, floods in the Philippines, earthquakes in Indonesia, a friend with cancer. It feels selfish to just chug along, enjoying her life. However, surrendering to total misery doesn't seem appropriate, either. Life, while you have it, is for living, surely? This human existence is a precious thing, not to be squandered. There seems no point dwelling in misery, so the writer decides to go on a cheery outing. It is one of the small pleasures of her life that two of her favourite things—the beach and the library—are right beside each other. Outside the library, two teenage boys sit talking, perched in the branch of a tree. The writer's spirits lift when she sees this simple happy thing: 'Two boys were sitting in a tree outside the library,' she jots in her notebook. It's a lovely simple sentence, and the writer knows just where it will go: in her book.

A ROSE PETAL CHAPTER

GLORY AWOKE, WITH no idea where she was. As she sat up, bewildered, the events of the previous day came flooding back in a jumble

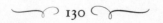

of remembering. The sun shone in the window as if nothing unusual had happened, which seemed to Glory most extraordinary. Miss Oleander stood in the doorway and, seeing the girl was awake, she came in with a tray on which sat a posy of daisies, a plum, and a bowl of chopped bread, sugar and milk.

'Breakfast, My Dear.'

Glory's eyes filled with tears at this kindness. When she was sick, her mother would prepare a tray of soothing invalid foods, such as baked milky puddings and lemon-honey water. Oh for the comfort of that life, which seemed so far away and long ago now.

Miss Oleander put the tray on the stool beside the bed and handed Glory a scrap of clean rag.

'Here, dry your eyes. I'll make us some tea.'

The food tasted delicious, as did the delicate liquid Miss Oleander poured from a silver pot into cups of finest pale green china.

'Rose petals, cornflowers and orange peel. A summery blend, do you like it?'

'Very much, thank you.'

'So, yesterday brought more than you bargained for?' Miss Oleander's deep blue eyes were kind yet serious.

'Indeed it did. I am frightened and confused. I learn that I am cursed to die, but then another thunderbolt arrives and I am offered a chance to live, for which I must thank you. Yet I know nothing of medicine nor magic. I don't know how to save a life, nor do I have any knowledge of any life that needs saving, other than my own.'

Glory's voice was desperate. Miss Oleander took her time before answering.

'A day such as yesterday will never come your way again. Yet come your way it has, like an unbidden tempest, as you say. Fear and confusion are to be expected, Child. However, whether you can understand it or not, things are unfolding exactly as they should.'

'How can you say so? I have been caught in a sticky net; one not of my own making. I am terrified by these strange machinations. Why should I be happy about my situation?'

'One would not expect you to be happy, but equanimity will serve you well. The past can't be undone but the future holds infinite possiblity.'

'So, what should I do?'

'You should get up, and bathe, and return to your duties. Events will unfold by themselves, you will see. You don't need to worry away at them like a rat chasing mustard seeds. When the time comes, you will know what to do.'

'How do *you* know? I do not mean to be impertinent, but I don't wish for dainty soothing words. If the future is mysterious, then how can you predict it and reassure me thus?'

'You'll have to trust me. Or rather, trust emergence, and the power of good to triumph over evil. I cannot see the future, not exactly, but I have some insight beyond those who have no arcane powers.'

Glory could think of no suitable reply. She looked into Miss Oleander's eyes, and the benevolence she saw there brought her a flicker of hope, though she was still in turmoil.

'Another plum?' Miss Oleander offered.

Glory was glad to be back amongst ordinary things. On a summery morning, in a world of plums and ball gowns, surely no harm could befall her?

'No, thank you. It was a delectable breakfast but I've taken sufficient. Shall I go to the princess, then?'

'Yes. The ball nears, and there will be much to attend to. Perhaps you will visit me again soon. You'll find I am here whenever you need me.'

When Glory returned to Princess Mirabella's chambers, she was greeted in a friendly fashion by a barefoot princess, dressed in a dusky-pink organza gown.

'The queen has told me of your plight. It is *most* alarming.' Mirabella looked up from the leather-bound book with snakeskin binding that she had been reading.

Glory gave her a wan smile. 'I am trying not to be too alarmed. The apothecary believes the circumstances of what I am to do shall appear to me in due course, and that there will be a good outcome. She advises me to take each ordinary day as it comes. So, here I am, Your Highness. Ready for duty.'

'It's good to see you alive and well. When you were missing, I was most distressed. As for Miss Oleander's advice, it sounds reasonable.' The princess tucked her feet into her rose velvet slippers and went to the window. 'Who would have thought that this very palace was the site of magic? I've become curious about the occult, and have been reading about spells. I wonder if I should attempt one myself? This book is full of devotions, divinations, purification rites, and enchantments. On St Agnes Eve, for instance, it's possible to dream of whom you will marry if two girls make a Dumbly Cake together, using eggshells as spoons, though the spell will be broken if either girl speaks.'

'I would prefer to stay away from magic of every kind, Your Highness, if you please. I've learnt it may lead to ill-fortune as easily as not...'

'Perhaps you are right. Some of these love spells are wondrous intriguing though. *Take a red rose. On the petals, write the name of the person you love, then dip the petals in fresh spring water gathered in the dawn. Throw the petals outside the house of the person you love.*'

'Do you think it would work?'

'It does seem a little fanciful. This one sounds more believable. *Take ten strands of your hair and two dozen hairs from the head of the person you wish to marry. Thread the hairs together while chanting these words: Tambour Chamber Marriage Kabana Kabuki Tuba. Burn the entwined hair.* Perhaps I might use this spell to enchant a husband, if I find a prince I like.'

'If I may be so bold, Your Highness, I thought you had no wish to be married.'

'True,' Mirabella admitted. 'Though if one did wish to marry, it would be best if one's love were reciprocated. My father has been extolling the virtues of the two sons of King Gilbert, whose kingdom is very wealthy. Apparently, the younger one, Prince Leonard, is handsome, and charming in every way, but his heart may already be taken by another.'

'And his older brother?'

'My father says Timothy is more likely to fall for my charms. He is a fine man, witty, gallant, and expert in falconry. A shame he is not as handsome as his brother.' Mirabella's eyes twinkled.

'Tis the first time I've seen her cheery, Glory realised. 'A pity. A fellow should be easy on the eye.'

'I agree.' The princess fell silent. Her thoughts turned to Arlo, who was very easy on the eye, indeed.

'Has your ball gown been altered to your satisfaction?' asked Glory, remembering her duties.

'It hasn't been delivered, but surely by now it's hemmed. Please fetch it, then I will try on my entire outfit. I'd like to ride this afternoon, so you could set out my riding outfit as well.'

'Certainly.' Glory made her way to Madame Star, the dressmaker, smiling tentatively. Strange magic afoot, indeed, that Princess Mirabella should be so mellow.

The Reader

〉 It's been a pretty good week. I got ninety-two per cent for my essay: *Saving the Planet One Penguin at a Time*. Mum finished knitting my rainbow-striped beanie. I like it. It looks cool. Next, she's going to knit a tea-cosy shaped like a house, for her friend Lillian, who's an architect. At school, Dylan and I have been kind of avoiding each other, but she hasn't thrown any crap at me. Life is heaps more relaxing without the D = Dire factor. It'll be interesting to see what goes down with Ms G on Thursday.

THE WRITER

The writer is not the person she'd hoped to be, which was someone elegant and serene. She writes four and a half sentences but doesn't like them much, so she visits her friend, instead. The friend, intelligent and intense, asks what the driving force of her book is. The writer rambles on about a fairy story... and the WF suggests some fine ideas, but somehow they don't seem right. It's hard to know what should go in her book and what should not. The writer farewells her friend and strolls by the river. How come she keeps forgetting the same simple truth? If she worries about it, the writing gets harder. If she fills her life with the fun stuff, creativity follows. 'Easy is right. Begin right and you are easy. Continue easy and you are right,' as Chuang Tsu said.

A CHAPTER
CONTAINING
TEA-LEAVES AND
SUGAR-DUSTED
INSECTS

ROLF USUALLY DID what bossy Mrs Blossom asked him to do, but today he couldn't face potatoes that required peeling and cabbages that needed shredding, so he told a small yet effective lie.

'My stomach isn't right.' He squeezed up his face, put one hand on his belly, and raised the other to his throat, as if both pooing and spewing were imminent.

'Good Lawd, Lad! Your timing is most exceptional inconvenient!' Mrs B was both exasperated and distracted. She was boning a quail (never an easy task) and with the hot flushes she was having that morning it was even more bothersome.

'I can't really spare you, but take a break if you

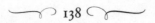

must. Go to the apothecary for a concoction to settle your innards, and come back t'kitchen when you're able.' Mrs Blossom returned to her pale, dead quail.

'Thank you, Ma'am.' Rolf scooped some sugar into his pocket, and scooted out the door and across the courtyard. Making sure no one was watching him, he sneaked through the blue door to his favourite hiding place.

Rolf loved the potting shed, with its neat seed beds and calm greenery. It was one of the few spots where he could find solitude, because he shared a room with Arlo, and there was always chatter in the busy kitchen. He pulled a few weeds out from amongst the radish seedlings, then shifted flowerpots until he unearthed a dead cricket. He stuck it in his pocket, where it joined a beetle carcass and three deceased flies.

Rolf made his way stealthily out of the potting shed, past the raspberry beds and through the oak trees to the stream. He sat down on a rock, carefully dusted each dead insect with sugar, and waited. Before long, a frog arrived, as he knew it would. The young man sat quietly, watching the frog eat. His thoughts had been very muddled of late. He was worried about Glory, and this perplexed him more than anything he'd ever experienced. Up until now, his life had been a quiet one. Born on the royal estate, he had lived as a child with his parents in a cottage nearby. Rolf's father had been head gardener at the palace, and his mother worked as a chambermaid. Sadly, they'd died of

scarlet fever when he was ten. It was a miracle, everyone said, that the skinny boy had lived. The palace
had become Rolf's home after the death of his parents.
Mrs Blossom made sure he was fed, but, in the main,
he had raised himself.

He had always felt a profound affinity for the
natural world. It contained everything: bright and
shadow, movement and stillness, beauty and horror.
Rolf relished the tranquillity of being alone in nature.
He never tired of observing the habits of birds, frogs,
bees, and other insects. They were his main com-
panions, and he felt no need to control or participate
in their tiny worlds — just observe, enjoy and learn.
But now! A red-haired girl with a moondust smile had
arrived, and Rolf was not used to the new thoughts
that wandered around his noggin on unruly paths.
Novel feelings and sensations arose in his body, some
pleasant, some alarming. The young man sat quietly,
watching the stream flow. So peaceful. Yet, at any
moment, a storm could bring sudden wild currents.
As in nature, so in life. Glory was in danger, possibly
mortal danger. Rolf would do anything to help her, but
he felt powerless over the strange forces at play. He
sighed and kicked a rock, scaring the frog back into
the water. Then he reluctantly made his way back to
the kitchen. He hoped Mrs Blossom wouldn't ask if
he'd seen the apothecary, because he wasn't willing to
fake illness to Miss Oleander, whose dark eyes knew

everything and more. Luckily for him, Mrs Blossom was engrossed at the kitchen table, having her teacup read by Lonely Jack, the wandering minstrel.

'That's right, Madame. Turn your cup counter-clockwise, three times, now tip it upside down.' The gypsy scratched his lank black hair with thin brown fingers, a gold scarab ring glinting.

Mrs Blossom tipped the white china cup upside down onto the saucer.

'Now turn it up t'right way again, and make a wish,' the gypsy instructed.

Rolf didn't hold Jack in much esteem. The scrawny fellow turned up once or twice a year with fancy wares to sell, songs to sing, and fortunes to tell. Everyone knew he was a shonky pedlar. There were floor sweepings in his black pepper, brick dust in his nutmeg, and his ribbons had already been worn, but his songs were jolly enough, and the gossip he carried from town to town earned him a cup of tea and a bite to eat wherever he went. Cooks and wives of the house greeted him cheerily, for every woman loves a fortune teller.

'Are you all right, Lad?' Mrs Blossom glanced up.

'Much better now, thank you. I visited the outhouse, and I seem to have come right.'

'Well, give your hands a scrub, then do the same to the potatoes. I'm busy here, as you can see.'

The cook turned away, keen to learn what her

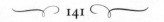

tea-leaves held. Lonely Jack didn't hurry. He took the cup and studied it slowly, turning it back and forth to look at the patterns from every angle.

'Ah,' he pronounced solemnly, drawing out the moment in a theatrical manner.

'What is it? What do you see?' Mrs Blossom asked eagerly.

The fellow is such a fake, thought Rolf. *He'll merely say what she wants to hear. It's plain trickery, that's what it is.*

'I think...yes, I see boats. Small boats. A boat can mean a journey. Are you planning a journey, Fair Lady?'

'I've not left this county since I were a girl, and I don't intend to. There's quite enough here in this very kitchen to keep me busy.'

'Interesting. Well, then, are you expecting visitors? Boats can signify visitors from far away.'

'Lawd, aren't you the one? That is most perpikashus, for the king and queen are hosting a ball, on the full moon, just four days away. High-ranking gentlemen are coming from near and far, for the princess is to choose a husband.'

'Ah,' pronounced Jack, as if he'd just learnt something of great import.

Everyone knows that, Rolf thought. *The scallywag will have heard all about it in the tavern. How could Mrs Blossom be so foolish? What nonsense will he spout next?*

'But there's more,' Jack continued ponderously.

''Tis a bottle, see, here? I thought at first it were a duck, which has an entirely different meaning, but no, I think you'll agree, Madame, it is a bottle, which concerns one's constitution. Has your health been deficient of late?'

'Good Sir, you are completely correct.' Mrs Blossom's bosom bounced with amazement and enthusiasm. 'I've been ever so poorly these last months. I can only muster the energy of a feather duster, some days, and I go from hot to cold and back again for no apparent reason. It is most disconcerty, and interferes with me work something chronic...'

A bottle, that would be right. Maybe if you stayed away from the bottle, your health would improve all by itself, Rolf commented inwardly.

The pedlar took a more sympathetic approach. 'Well, Dear Lady, I advise you to visit the apothecary, in that case, for you can never be too careful in these delicate matters. I have heard that — for women who are not, shall we say, in the first flush of youth — a herbal tonic can produce results most efficacious.'

'I shall do as you say. Indeed I thank you. Here, this is for you.' Mrs Blossom fossicked in the pocket of her apron until she found a silver coin amongst the buttons, corks and rumpled kerchiefs. The pedlar smiled his sly smile and turned to Rolf, who was hard at work scrubbing the rather ancient potatoes.

'How about you, Young Man? Would you care to

see the future? I'd be happy to read your palm, or your teacup, before I go on my way.'

'I think n —' But before Rolf had time to refuse, Mrs Blossom answered for him.

'Don't be bothering with him. Our Rolf is a man of science, he don't believe in such things, plus he don't have a coin in his pocket, do you, Lad? There be only a dead beetle or a old peppermint in his trouser pocket, I think you'll find. Hurry yourself up, Boy, for I need them potatoes, and chop them carrots while you're at it. 'Tis time I got back to work and all; the joint won't cook itself.'

Lonely Jack made as if to go, yet he lingered in the doorway until Mrs Blossom took her cue.

'Here, take some walnuts and a slice of my lardy cake. Now, be on your way, Good Fellow.'

'You look beautiful,' Glory told Mirabella, and it was true. The green silk gown clung to the princess's body, accentuating the curve of her waist and her rounded hips. The sapphires and diamonds of the Magic Blossom Tiara twinkled and glinted, the green dancing slippers fitted like a dream.

'All I need now is jewellery. I found nothing suitable in my casket, but I'll ask Mama to choose something from her collection.' Mirabella stood by the window, gazing out, trying not to feel sad about her future. 'Hey, you! Wait!' she cried in a rather unseemly manner.

'Glory, run down to the courtyard. The fortune-telling pedlar known as Lonely Jack is about. I want to see him. Fetch him, if you please.'

THE WRITER

Spending months in front of a screen is taking a toll on the writer's body. Her arm aches and her eyes itch. Her brain hurts, too. All the plot lines in her story are crowding her, like so many fabric squares inside her head that need to be sewn into a complicated quilt. It's daunting and confusing, and it's making her cranky. Why didn't she become a chef, a film-maker or an interior designer, or train for a proper job, like a librarian or optometrist, that has sick pay, and regular pay packets, and a Christmas party? But she can't stop now. She can't just abandon her characters: dear Rolf, frightened Glory, funny old Mrs Blossom and scruffy Elda. She's become fond of Princess Mirabella and her hapless parents. If the writer doesn't continue, there will be no dinner tonight in the palace, and the curse will remain unbroken. The kingdom will go to rack and ruin, Rolf's grandchildren will not invent the deckchair, the coiled spring, and the fountain pen. Having brought her characters to life, the writer must now take them where they need to go. Otherwise, it would be like killing your children, and that would never do...

The Reader

》 Ms G was wearing a green hoodie, green velvet trousers, and a t-shirt bearing the slogan *There is no Planet B*.

'Come on in, Nova.'

'I like your outfit,' I said, looking round her office. Dylan wasn't there yet. The little statue was, though, with a fresh pink rosebud by her feet.

'Really?' Ms G grinned. 'I threw this lot on this morning in great haste and have spent the rest of the day wondering if it was too Robin Hood...'

'I like it.'

'Dylan's not here yet, as you can see. She *is* at school today, do you think?'

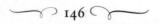

'Yeah. I saw her in class this morning.'

'I guess she'll be here soon then.'

I went over to the window to take a closer look at Kuan Yin. She had a certain radiance, with her dainty ivory smile

'Are you Buddhist, then?' I asked, for lack of anything better.

'I'm not really any sort of "ist", actually. How about you?'

'I'm not any sort of "ist", either. My mum was brought up Methodist, but she doesn't go to church these days. Dad's parents were Quakers. He goes to meetings occasionally. They try and live a good life, though.'

'That's the main thing, isn't it? I try to live by what the Dalai Lama said: My religion is kindness.'

'Can't beat that,' I agreed, trying to sound perky even though I felt crap. Dylan not showing up is like a kick in the guts. It's embarrassing that she can't even be bothered coming.

'So, how's your week been?' Ms G plonked herself down on the sofa and offered me the red wicker chair.

'Pretty good. My mum knitted me a hat.' I sounded lame so I hurried onwards. 'I'm reading a good book. It's kind of a fairytale. There's a curse on a girl called Glory. I'm keen to find out what happens to her...' I was still lost in the land of lame, but Ms G didn't seem to mind.

'Isn't it good when you've got a book to hide in? It's one of my favourite things, when life lets me down. Speaking of let-downs, it looks like Dylan isn't going to show. How do you feel about that?'

'Pretty crap.'

'Understandable. Did you two have a play date?'

'Yep. I went to her house. We made cards. It was fun, actually. We haven't talked at school, but she's left me alone, which is a big improvement.'

'Good on you. Look, I'll chase up Dylan and ask her to get in touch with you. Meanwhile, you think up the next activity, okay?'

'I'm not keen.' I sounded sullen, but I didn't care. 'If Dylan can't be arsed showing up, why should I bother?'

'I don't blame you for being peeved, Nova. I would be too. But Dylan's got a lot on her plate. She isn't coping with her father's serious illness. Maybe give her another chance, if I can sort it?'

'I suppose so.'

'Good on you, kiddo. Okay, you are officially free to go. Enjoy that hat!'

I trudge home, feeling stink. I put on my pyjamas and my hat, eat some cold potatoes out of the fridge, and scan the TV Guide, but there's nothing on except the kid's shows, and nothing good on tonight, either. It's all forensics, unless you want to watch *Britain's Worst Teeth*. I feel very, very tragic. It's under the duvet for me, with Mirabella and Glory.

A CHAPTER
CONTAINING
FURTHER DOINGS
OF A SOMEWHAT
DODGY CHARACTER

THE COURTYARD WAS A HIVE of bustle and commotion with preparations for the grand ball. Groomsmen rolled kegs of ale across the cobblestones, gardeners deadheaded roses and tidied hedges, yard boys raked gravel, and Elda and Arlo chased a squawking turkey which had escaped and was avoiding its destiny of the pot. Finally, Glory spotted the pedlar. He was leaning against the ivy wall, eyeing a winsome chambermaid as she thumped a willow stick on a dusty rug which was hanging on a rope clothesline.

'Tis no wonder he's known as Lonely Jack, Glory thought to herself, for his skin was badly pocked with

old craters as well as new pustules, and his eyes were shifty.

'My mistress, Princess Mirabella, wishes you to accompany me to her chambers.'

'Gladly.' Jack winked at the chambermaid, who blushed and gave the carpet an extra hard whack.

'You're new, aren't you? Ain't seen you here before,' the pedlar remarked jauntily as he followed Glory up the grand staircase leading off the entrance foyer.

Glory nodded.

'How do you like working for the princess, then? They say she's a difficult one, but you look like the sort of lass who could take anything in her stride.'

Glory could think of no suitable reply, and she didn't like the pedlar's slippery tone so she ignored him and made haste along the corridor.

'Oh, hoity-toity me.' Lonely Jack realised he had no chance with this young beauty, so he contented himself with the thought of the gold coin that was sure to come his way once he'd read the royal fortune.

As Glory and the pedlar entered the royal chambers, Princess Mirabella rose from her high-backed, gilded chair. She'd been writing at her tortoiseshell writing table.

Lonely Jack bowed low. 'At your service, Your Royalty,' he said, hoping it was the correct greeting.

The princess nodded, even though it wasn't, and

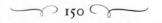

placed her quill beside the gleaming inkpot.

Solid gold, by the look, Jack noted. Pity he couldn't slip that in his pocket, for it would fetch a handsome price.

'I wish you to tell the fortune of myself and my maid, Glory. You do read palms, do you not?'

Jack hesitated a moment before replying. He didn't read palms but perhaps he could pretend to, since it was what the princess wanted. On second thoughts, it probably wasn't the best plan. The pedlar had heard that, though the princess was a difficult young woman, she was intelligent.

'I'm sorry, Your Royalty, I am not trained in palmistry, or chiromancy, as it is also known. My speciality is reading tea-leaves. I learnt it from my grandmother, a Romany whose skill was known in counties far and wide. My abilities do not match my grandmother's, but I do have some aptitude in the ancient art of reading the teacups, and I am at your service, Your Royalty.'

'Very well then, but please dispense with calling me Your Royalty, there's no need for it,' said the princess, who was beginning to wonder if the whole thing was a good idea. The pedlar seemed rather oily, but since they had come this far... 'Proceed, then,' she instructed crisply.

'We will need a teapot and two cups, if you please.'

'My breakfast tray is still here, though the tea is cold. There's only one cup though ... no, wait, we could use the pretty cups from the tea set in my bureau of antiquities, could we not?'

'Certainly,' replied Jack, eyeing up the contents of the cupboard, a veritable treasure trove of antiques and curiosities, the likes of which he had never seen.

Contrary to Rolf's assumption, though the pedlar had dubious morals, he was not a complete fake. He *had* learnt the ancient art of reading tea-leaves from his grandmother, whose predictions oft came true with uncanny precision. Jack's own forecasts were not quite as accurate, but he had studied the meanings of the symbols, and had faith in prophecy.

The circumstances the fortune teller now found himself in were not ideal. The correct Romany procedure was to make a fresh brew of hot tea and pour it, studying the client's face and mannerisms as they drank, but in this case, Jack took the easy road. He sat the young ladies down, poured them each a small amount of tea, and began.

'Since the tea is cold, it's not necessary to drink an entire cup. If you would each take three swallows, that will suffice.'

Princess Mirabella and Glory did as he asked, then Jack poured the excess tea back into the pot, leaving only tea-leaves in each cup.

'Would Your Highness care to go first?'

Mirabella nodded, and Jack instructed her to place the cup on the upturned saucer, just as he'd shown Mrs

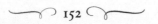

Blossom. Again, the pedlar took his time and viewed the leaves carefully from every angle before he spoke.

'There is only one symbol here, which is unusual, but it means that the sign is a portentous one . . .'

'Yes, yes, go on!' Mirabella said impatiently.

'It's a bee. See here, near the handle. A bee is most fortuitous, Your Royalty,' said Jack, in his eagerness forgetting the princess's instruction. 'It denotes prosperity, the acquisition of fortune, the gaining of wealth through trade. A bee is a very happy thing to find in a teacup, indicating a change of fortune for the good.'

'Really? Are you certain of it?' Mirabella asked sharply. As far as she was concerned, the reading was *bad* news. It confirmed the fate she was dreading. She was to be married off to a prosperous husband, for the sake of her parent's fortune. There was to be no escape from the fate she dreaded.

'I am certain.' Jack was puzzled. He'd expected a more cheerful response. The rumours proved true; the princess was a hard person to please, and no mistake about it.

'Glory?' Mirabella went to the window and cast her gaze past gardens and forest to the sky beyond; the blue sky of freedom that would never be hers. Glory hesitated. She also found Jack distasteful. His manner was obsequious, yet the uncertainty of her future ate into her, like a rat gnawing hard cheese. It couldn't hurt, could it, to find out which way the wind would blow? She made a small curtsey, sat down in the carved elm chair the princess had vacated, and followed the ritual.

It seemed to Glory that this time Jack took even longer to pronounce her fortune, and she was correct. It was the part of the job that the pedlar liked the least, for what he saw in the cup before him were bad omens. He'd learnt the hard way that, when you cast an ill fortune, the client oft became truculent and did not cross your palm with a decent amount of silver. His grandmother had instructed him to tell the truth and tell it straight, but Jack was made of a different mettle. Finally, he set the cup down and smiled his devious smile at Glory.

'Have you ever had your fortune told before, Young Miss?'

Glory shook her head and waited. The first dark shape Jack saw in her cup was the Ace of Spades. It represented sorrow and hindrance, and Aces are cards of great significance. Close by was a configuration in the shape of the gallows, which signified extreme danger.

'See here, 'tis a cloud,' said Jack, pointing to the Ace of Spades.

'What does a cloud mean?'

'You're facing a dark period, but the problem will eventually blow away on the winds of change,' Jack said, hoping he sounded convincing.

'What's the other symbol?' Mirabella leant over Glory's shoulder, having returned to observe the reading.

'That one ... I'm in two minds about it,' said Jack,

stalling for time. 'I think it be a lock. Yes, 'tis a lock, which means an obstacle, a difficult problem that needs solving.'

'It doesn't look like a lock to me,' Mirabella said crossly. Suddenly she wanted the man gone, with his crafty manner and his stupid predictions.

'What does your ladyship think it resembles?' asked Jack quickly.

'It looks more like a gallows,' said Mirabella, who, seeing Glory's shocked pallor, immediately regretted her forthright words.

'A gallows? Actually, I do believe you are correct.' Jack didn't contradict the princess. In fact he was relieved by her accuracy, for he'd lacked the bravery to deliver the truth, but since it had not come from him he was now free to offer an appropriate warning.

'When a gallows appears in a reading, it means there is great danger. Every action and impulse must be weighed most carefully.'

'Does it mean death?' Glory asked in a whisper.

'Not always death, no . . . but it does indicate impending trouble. I would advise extreme caution on your part.'

'Indeed,' Mirabella said sharply. 'You may go. Visit the head butler on your way out and ask him to give you a small coin for your troubles.'

Jack bowed low and slunk from the room. It was not what he'd hoped for. Despite his best efforts, the princess was displeased, and there'd not be much point passing this way again.

Glory and Mirabella sat quietly after the fortune teller had gone. Each needed time to digest their readings, and neither was keen to believe or discuss the ominous reading the pedlar had cast for Glory.

'Well?' the princess finally asked. 'What say you to this swarthy gypsy and his pronouncements?'

'It is confusing. My two symbols seemed to contradict each other, and he seemed ... a trifle shifty perhaps?'

'I agree. Let's cast him from our minds. I'm keen to ride, so lay out my outfit, if you please. And, whilst I am riding, perhaps you could find Mama and arrange for me to look at the jewellery this afternoon?' Mirabella spoke gently. Knowing that her maid had the weight of the world on her shoulders had softened her heart.

'Gladly.' The cloud of Glory's life held one small silver lining, for at this stormy time the princess's new kindness was a welcome blessing. Everything else was evil weather.

THE WRITER

Why did she choose to write <u>this</u> book, with its interweaving plot lines and need for

complexity? Why not a linear narrative about a princess in a tower who starts out innocent and lovely, writes beautiful poetry, but then turns bad and becomes a lesbian vampire killer? Or else a TV show, with scary scenes and heaps of clever humour, that gains a cult following and pays big money. The writer can't work out how Glory is going to save a life. She wanders around aimlessly, thinking about possible deaths. Hanging? Suicide? Poison? She really hopes no one can hear her mumbling to herself. Perhaps Glory must die.

In her spare time, the writer is practising green dharma, the essence of which is to stop shopping. This is hard, as she's always loved buying quirky stuff from op shops. Not shopping exposes chasms of longing, but also brings a strange peacefulness. She'd hoped to become as rich and famous as JK Rowling, although apparently JK Rowling considered breaking her own arm when she was behind deadline on the fourth <u>Harry Potter</u>. The writer's desires have mellowed. 'I don't mind that I don't have squillions,' she says to herself. 'I shall dine like a queen on fabulous soup, walk on the beach at sunset, and be simple and ordinary and happy.'

The Reader

> I am peed off, pooed off, cranky, grumpy, shitty, cross, unhappy, and totally frigging miserable. I think that just about sums it up. How mortifying that Dylan didn't even bother to come to counselling. I secretly hoped we might become friends. That's how pathetic I am, wanting someone who treats me badly to be my friend. I am tragic, for sure. Even reading is not comforting me at present. Now Mirabella and Glory are getting along nicely, in the book, but in my life nothing is going nicely. I am lonely, and nobody likes me.

CHAPTER
SEVENTY- SEVEN
AND SIX
SEVENTHS

LORY PUT AWAY Mirabella's slippers, plumped the fat duck-feather pillows on the sumptuous royal bed, and smoothed the satin quilt. Then she sat down on the seat in the bay window. She'd never felt more alone in her life. Below, in the courtyard, she spied Rolf and Elda returning from the garden, carrying baskets of carrots and fresh herbs. The sight of her two friends smiling and chatting brought a strange sorrow to Glory's heart because, amongst the tumble of her thoughts and feelings of late, there was an important thing she'd only just admitted, even to herself. *I have a liking for Rolf.* Yes, now she had said it. Not only that, but it seemed to Glory that Rolf had a liking for her. He was a quiet young man, and kind to everyone, but she did not think she'd misunderstood the sweetness of his feelings towards her. Yet now Glory's mind was so tormented that she could only imagine the worst. *How can I halt what fate has in store for me? How could I ever save a life? I am but a dewdrop on a stem, a snowdrop in a vast field, and my time is running out. There are only four more nights until the full moon. I see no chance. I shall die, and that is that.* Glory smiled a sad smile that held no humour, and cast her gaze back to the courtyard just in time to see Elda trip on a stone, sending carrots tumbling to the ground. Rolf stooped to help gather them and Glory noticed his hand brush Elda's as they reached for the final carrot. Then, together, the pair continued their merry way across the yard. *They will marry, when I am gone.* The thought hit Glory, sharp as a spider bite. *They will live quietly in a cottage and be happy. Elda will make cheese to sell at market, Rolf will write a book about insects. Their dear little babies will be named Daisy, Fred and Albert. If my name is ever mentioned, they will say, yes, how sad it were about Glory. Apart from that, I will be entirely forgotten.* Glory wiped the tears from her cheeks with her sleeve. *I must go and see the queen about Mirabella's jewellery. Someone must be happy. Perhaps it will be the princess, for it surely won't be me.*

Mirabella rode up hill and down dale, across the wide fields spread out before her like the velvety green cloak of a giant. How she wished she could keep riding for ever; gallop away from duty and demand. But, despite her longing, Mirabella was royal through and through, and she knew that her idle wish could never come true. Where would she go and how would she live? Word of her escape would spread throughout the kingdom. She would be hunted down, found and taken back to the palace. There was nothing for it but to face her destiny.

She cantered back to the stables, handed the leather bridle to the groomsman who stood ready to brush Oak's coat, and made her way back to her chamber. Glory was nowhere to be seen, but on the dressing table was a set of jewels. Mirabella took out the necklace. She hung the dainty tumble of sparkling diamonds and glittering emeralds around her neck; held a matching earring to her ear. They looked wonderful, even with her riding outfit. Despite her misgiving about the future, the princess was pleased that at least her outfit for the ball was enchanting, and complete.

THE WRITER

The writer has written three-quarters of her book, and finally it begins to flow. It's like doing a big jigsaw puzzle; utterly chaotic at first, but if you keep going, tiny piece by tiny piece, at a certain point the shape emerges. You can see where the gaps are and which bits you need to fill the holes. Each morning before getting to work, the writer walks. As she walks, the jigsaw pieces arrive. It's as if God, or the universe, or the magic pen in the sky is sending her ideas, scenes, entire dialogues, to fit into her book. Meanwhile, her own life takes place around and between Mrs Blossom's kitchen, Mirabella's horse riding, and Glory's destiny. It makes the writer dreamy, to live in both worlds. She's prone to dropping stuff, forgetting things, and wearing earrings that don't match her cardigan.

The Reader

❭ I don't know who I am anymore. Beth is a vegan, Rada plays guitar, Gerald is a rich smart-arse. I used to be Nova, the interesting girl whose dad brought cool lollies from America and a kimono from Japan, but now I'm just floating in a lonely sky of blerk.

I've been hiding upstairs, generally wallowing in misery. When the phone rings, I can't even be bothered answering it. I'm sick of myself, and hungry, so I go downstairs, only to find Mum on the phone, sounding agitated.

'Everything? No way! Have you talked to the airline? Okay, right. Yeah. Okay, I'll get onto it. Ring me back in half an hour, okay?' She puts down the phone, face scrunched up.

'Whassup?'

'All your father's luggage has gone missing. So far, the airline can't track it; it could be anywhere between Cairo and the UK. He's stuck in London with only the clothes he's wearing. There's an important meeting in the morning, and he hasn't got a suit. I have to find some stuff, like a copy of the travel insurance. Could you get the tea, Petal? I'm starving.'

'Yep. I'm starving, too. What's to eat?'

'Cold chicken and salad, and some of that nice pane de casa bread you like.'

'No worries, Mum.' I get out two big white plates, put beetroot, capers and olives on top of some greens, grab myself a quarter chicken, some OJ, and two slices of bread slathered with pesto. Mum's back on the phone, so I leave her dinner on the bench and take mine upstairs on a tray. Which I nearly drop when I get into my bedroom because...

A CHAPTER CONTAINING VARIOUS EXCITING EVENTS AND SEVERAL ADJECTIVES

MIRABELLA CHANGED FROM her riding costume into her most comfortable dress, a soft yellow sateen. She was halfway through writing a note to her cousin but then remembered she'd be seeing Imogen at the ball. The princess felt a tiny bit of excitement. Perhaps there *would* be some young man who'd catch her fancy; someone worthy of her affections. But where was her maid? She must have gone on some small errand, and would shortly reappear.

It was nearly noon, and Mirabella was famished after her long ride. Usually, she took her lunch in her chamber, but when Glory didn't return the princess slipped on her white pumps embroidered with tiny daisies and went in search of sustenance. On her way down the long corridor, Arlo appeared, carrying a silver urn of sweet lilac and trailing ivy.

'Have you seen my maid?'

'No, I have not. May I be of any service, Your Highness?' Arlo bowed low. The princess looked very pretty in her summery outfit. At night, Arlo dreamt about the princess, for indeed he did have a fancy for her, but he also had a fancy for Rolf, which was most confusing for him. One person Arlo did not have a fancy for was Veronica, the daughter of the baker, to whom he was betrothed, but that was another story entirely.

'You can, actually. I'm going to the kitchen. If my maid's not there, fetching my lunch, you must try to find her.'

Arlo hastily set the flowers on a nearby plinth and followed Mirabella to the kitchen. Elda was churning butter, and Rolf was washing pots, but Mrs Blossom was nowhere to be seen. After some chit-chat it transpired that Mrs Blossom was *indisposed,* and no one knew where Glory was, so Rolf got busy making lunch for the princess, while Elda and Arlo were despatched to find Glory.

'I hope this will suffice, Your Highness?' Rolf had

set a tray with silver cutlery, a linen napkin, a goblet, and a platter containing fresh bread, a curl of creamy butter, several thick slices of beef, a saucer of walnut chutney, and a juicy, ripe peach.

'It is not my usual fare. It resembles a ploughman's feast, but yes, it will do well enough. However, I'm thirsty after my morning's riding. I require some elder-flower cordial.'

'Yes, Your Highness. I'll fetch some from the cellar.'

The princess waited impatiently. She wanted to grab the peach and devour it, but it wasn't very royal to stand in a kitchen eating fruit with her fingers. Once more, Mirabella longed to be a commoner. After what seemed like a very long time, Rolf reappeared.

'I'm very sorry, Your Highness. There was no elder-flower cordial to be found, but perhaps this would be to your liking?' He held out a tall clear bottle filled with a pale pink liquid.

'What is it?'

'It's a light wine made from berries. A summery drink, very tasty, so they say.'

'Very well. I shall take my repast in the rose garden. Bring my tray, if you please, and send my maid to me as soon as she's found. Her habit of disappearing is becoming somewhat tiresome.'

Glory sat on her bed, weeping. All her troubles had knocked her flat. Now that she'd begun to cry, she couldn't stop. She was frightened and heart-weary. She longed for her mother, three days' journey and another lifetime away.

Elda searched the library, the potting shed, the out-house, the vegetable garden, the dressmaker's studio, and the infirmary, with no success. She climbed upstairs towards the attic slowly, partly because she had a blister on her little toe and partly because she didn't expect to find Glory there. However, she was worried that her friend had packed her suitcase and run away from the palace, so she wanted to check that Glory's few belongings were still in their bedroom. On finding her dear chum sobbing on the bed, Elda sat down and soothed her as best she could.

'There there, there there, my little dumpling.' Elda's mother had used these words, so Elda said them, even though they sounded a bit silly. Glory thought so, too. She sat up and managed a smile.

'Little dumpling indeed.'

'My mama used to say it when I were ill...'

'I almost wish *I* were ill. I think it would be better than carrying on with this dreadful unknowing,' Glory said in despair.

Elda was completely out of her depth with the enormity of the situation, but she did her best.

'You mustn't wish for ill health, for it might bring further bad luck upon you. It would be wiser not to dwell on your troubles, I reckon, but to get on with the day, like Miss Oleander suggested. The princess is looking for you. She came to the kitchen to fetch her own lunch.'

'Is she angry?'

'Not yet, but I'd wager she's heading in that direction...'

'Bless you, Elda. I shall go and attend to my duties.'

The pair hurried downstairs and dashed across the courtyard, where Arlo spotted them.

'I've been looking for you two. The princess is lunching in the rose garden and she's asking for her maid. And Mrs Blossom wants Elda back.'

'Is Rolf in the kitchen?' Glory wanted to ask. She suddenly longed to see him, but the life of a servant girl does not allow one to follow one's heart when one wishes, so she made her way to the rose garden.

The Reader

〉...because there, with her bum half out my window, is Dylan. Now I know the true meaning of the word 'gobsmacked'.

'Oh bugger!' Dylan reluctantly climbs back inside. 'I don't suppose there's much point doing a bunk?'

'You bet there isn't. What on earth are you doing here?'

'I'm running away.' She's wearing a classic burglar outfit—black jeans, black sneakers and a black hoodie—and she's clutching two supermarket bags of my stuff.

'So you thought you'd steal my things first. Nice.'

'I know, I know. Call the cops, tell your mother, whatever . . .'

Just then, I hear Mum calling up the stairs. 'Nova, I have to go out to fax something. I won't be long.'

'Okay,' I yell back. Then I turn to Dylan. 'Sit. Talk. What's going on?' I grab the bags from her and look through them. My jeans, my two best tops, the Issey Miyake perfume Dad bought me duty-free, a Sharon Creech book, and my make-up purse. Dylan may be a thief, but she's got good taste. She sits down on the floor, leans against the wall, and starts to cry.

'Cut the waterworks.' My heart is hard. This girl is bad news, for sure.

Dylan snivels a bit more, then her story tumbles out. Her parents are away for a fortnight because her father is having some new treatment at a big hospital in Melbourne. They've employed a housekeeper, a ditzy cow in her thirties. Dylan hates her. She can't cope with any of it, so she decided to take off. She didn't want the police to know what clothes she was wearing so she decided to nick some of mine. Her story tapers out, and she starts picking pathetically at that dry skin around her fingernails.

'How do you know where I live?'

'Phone book.'

'Why me? I thought ... who cares what I thought. Why me?'

'I don't know. I'm not thinking straight. I just wanted to get away from that stupid woman; get away from everything. You wear cool stuff, and we're the same size ...'

'What a frigging compliment.' I'm angry with her but manage to muster a morsel of compassion. 'You can't outrun your troubles,' I say, sounding way wiser than I feel. 'Where are you going to go? What are you going to do? They'll just find you and haul you back. Plus, your parents don't need this kind of worry. It's pretty selfish of you to load them with another drama to deal with, if you ask me.'

'I didn't ask you, actually.'

'Well, you're in my bedroom trying to rip me off, so I think I've got a right to an opinion.'

'Fair enough,' she admits, defeated.

'Will the housekeeper—what's her name, by the way—will she have rung the cops yet?'

'Nah, she probably doesn't even know I've gone. Madeleine, Maddy for short. She is kind of a maddy, actually. She can't cook, hardly eats anything, borderline anorexia I reckon. She's a neat freak with no discernible sense of humour. She just tidies up relentlessly, then watches crime shows and stuff like *We Built a House in Tuscany But Now It's Falling Down*. She thinks I've gone to bed.'

'Right, here's what we're going to do. You are going to go home and stay home. If she susses you've been out and asks where, tell her you had to pick up some homework from a friend's place. And tomorrow, at school, you go straight to see Ms G. You have to tell her what's happened, Dylan. You need her help, for sure.'

She looks up from her cruddy fingernails and gives me a listless smile.

'Okay. Thanks, Nova. I'll do it, I promise. It's a good plan.'

'What's your phone number at home? I'm going to ring you in half an hour and make sure you're there. If you're not, I'm telling the housekeeper and my mother, and the shit will hit the fan.'

She scribbles her number on the back of an envelope that's sticking out of my rubbish bin, and heads towards the window.

'You can go out the door if you want,' I say, and we walk down together. I watch her jog off down the quiet, tree-lined street. Great timing, because Mum drives up almost as soon as Dylan turns the corner onto the main road.

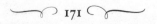

'What are you doing out here?' she asks, climbing out of the car. 'Look, I bought ice-cream. The good stuff.'

'Maple and pecan?'

'Yep.'

We sit in the kitchen and hoe in; one big bowl and two spoons. Sublime. I don't tell her I've still got my untouched dinner waiting for me upstairs.

'Your father's all sorted—well, as sorted as he can be. Hopefully, his luggage will turn up soon. I remember waiting for my lost bag in Florence. I sat in the garden of our pensione all day, wearing a big t-shirt, watching a tortoise wander around. Dad brought rolls, and tomatoes, and cheese for lunch, and red wine. In the evening, the bag turned up in a taxi. It was our most relaxing day in Europe.'

'Cool. Mum, did you ever have a toxic friend?'

'What do you mean by toxic?'

'Not sure, actually. Difficult, I guess. Someone troubled but who turned out to be worth the effort?'

'Well, there was Gillian. She turned out to be a . . . challenge.'

I remember Mum's friend Gill. We saw a lot of her when I was little. I liked her. She wore stripes with florals with spots, and arty brooches, and big scarves. Her house was messy and colourful, and she had a collection of little elephant statues made of wood, and ivory, and china.

'Yeah, you don't see her any more. How come?'

'We had heaps of fun together at uni. She was frisky and playful. We always kept in touch and enjoyed each other, over the years, but when her marriage broke up she got kind of ... whingeing and needy, I suppose. I tried to listen and be there for her, but it got pretty draining. The oddest thing was, just when I'd plucked up courage and was going to talk to her about the state of our friendship, she sent me the most horrid email ...'

'Like what?'

'A whole list of things she felt *I'd* done wrong over the years. Good that she got it all off her chest, but it was pretty twisted and cruel. I never wrote back, and that was that.'

'Did you miss her?'

'Yes and no. I missed the good old days, but not the whingeing. It was time to move on, for both of us, I guess. Why do you ask, Hon?'

'There's a girl at school, Dylan ...'

'The one who was giving you a hard time?'

'Yeah. Things have changed a bit ...' I'm about to tell Mum the whole saga, but something stops me, and then the phone rings again, and the moment passes. After Mum gets off the phone, I phone Dylan. She answers straight away.

'I'm here. Thanks for not dobbing me in, Nova.'

'You will go and see Ms G, won't you?'

'Yep, I promise.'

'Night then.'

When I get off the phone I feel a strange mixture of emotions: anger, weariness, pity, and something almost like love.

THE WRITER

Just as she establishes a nice smooth rhythm, the writer's work is interrupted by the coming of Christmas. It's alarming! There are cards to send, provisions to buy, gifts to wrap, shops to avoid, people to see, emails aplenty, ten pipers piping, three frogs a'wooing, and a partridge in a pear tree. The writer has a major disaster making her Christmas cake, but that's another story. Domestic goddess status is too hard, she decides, as she faces her own holy trilogy: a book deadline, a sore back, and the rapid onset of the festive season. Her orderly life tumbles like a box of baubles. The writer worries and frets, advances and retreats, sulks and finally surrenders.

She accepts that it's possible to both love and despise this nutty time of capitalism and chaos, abandons her writing until the New Year, and wombles onwards, a piece of dark fruitcake in one hand, a bowl of cherries in the other.

CHAPTER CONTAINING MERRIMENT, LIFE, AND DEATH

IRABELLA WAS GRUMPY. At first she'd taken pleasure in the dappled sunshine, the pretty roses, and her delicious victuals, but now she was thirsty, and hot, and bothery. Try as she might, she couldn't budge the cork in the bottle Rolf had given her. She scooped a little water from the fountain to wet her lips, but the soggy leaf floating in the water gave her cause to doubt the wisdom of drinking it.

'Where is that dratted girl?' she asked aloud.

'I'm here,' replied Glory, appearing through an archway in the yew hedge.

Mirabella regretted the 'dratted', but Glory did not seem to have taken offence.

'I am sorry to have kept you waiting, Your Highness.' Glory offered no explanation, but curtsied low.

Mirabella nodded her head slowly and elegantly, like a swan, as if to say *I will forgive your absence if you ignore my calling you 'dratted'.*

'Please open this, if you are able. I am parched.' The princess held out the bottle.

Glory gave the cork a few hard tugs, and out it came with a satisfying pop. She poured some into the goblet, and the princess drank it rapidly.

'How delectable.' Mirabella kicked off her slippers and wriggled her toes. 'I wanted elderflower cordial, but there was none to be found. This is a concoction made from berries,' she said, suddenly feeling a lot more cheerful. 'I do believe I can taste sunshine in it, as well as raspberries and a hint of rose petals. Pour me some more, if you please.' Glory did as she was asked and sat nearby, under a hanging bough of wisteria.

'Would *you* care for some of this delicious beverage?' the princess offered unexpectedly. There was only one goblet, and Glory knew a chambermaid should not drink from the same vessel as a princess, but the day was hot and the offer was tantalising, so she nodded.

'Here, fill it to the brim and come sit by me. Let's

drink this taste of summer together.' The princess wriggled her toes some more, and giggled, for no real reason. Really, this fruity fizz was proving most delightful. It was not long before Glory also felt the benefits of this most efficacious brew. All her troubles floated gently away. The two young women laughed and talked of ball gowns and baubles, but, as the bottle emptied and the afternoon wore on, the conversation turned to more serious matters.

'This magical wine has cheered me greatly, but our lives will still await us tomorrow.' The princess sighed.

'If I may say so, your life seems to be a desirable one, Your Highness.' The wine had loosened Glory's tongue. Since she was facing her own death, there seemed little point in niceties and falsehood.

The princess did not seem troubled by Glory's honesty. 'It may seem that way to you, but… the truth is that I am trapped, and it makes me feel wretched,' she replied.

'But surely you have everything a person could want? A fine palace, delicious foods, the best medicines when you are ill, servants who attend to your every desire…'

'These things provide pleasure of a certain kind, it is true, and no doubt I could be more grateful for it. Yet in my heart I'm lonely and sad. My life is that of a caged bird, even though my cage is wondrously gilded.'

'I see it differently, if I may say so, Your Highness. For are we not all caged in some way?'

'Royalty is a rare kind of prison, but it is a prison, no less. Common folk may marry whom they wish, choose their own occupation, kiss whatever boy they like. They do not have to suffer the eyes of the world upon them.'

'It may seem like a life of freedom to you, but we are all bound by conditions, Your Highness. Some are bound by poverty, some by illness, and we are all bound by the restrictions of our society. I myself would like to be a landowner, but this is only allowed to men.'

'Yes, it is as you say. I see through my own eyes...it's good to glimpse the world through yours. One's own troubles always seem the most important.' The princess sighed again, then continued. 'At least my lot is not as bad as poor Queen Claude's. She was betrothed, when she was but six years old, to her cousin. She wed at fourteen and gave birth to seven royal children. She was only twenty-four when she died, utterly exhausted, or épuisée, as they say.'

'That's horrid beyond belief.'

'Oh, but let's not dwell on serious things. Let's cast dark clouds aside, including that hornswoggler of a gypsy and his ridiculous fortunes. We must not waste such a lovely evening. What say you to a stroll along the stream?'

THE WRITER

After the fruitcake and the frolics, the tinsel and the tears, the new year begins. The writer is worried that the paper world she's created may have thinned and vanished, but, no, it's still there. Despite the summery call of the beach, the pile of books beside her bed, and the dear friends who want to have a cuppa, the writer closes her door. She has a deadline. Douglas Adams said, 'I love deadlines. I especially love the whooshing sound they make as they go flying by,' but the writer is keen not to hear that whooshing sound. She sits for ages, waiting for something to occur. As Stephen Leacock remarked, 'Writing is not hard. Just sit down and write it as it occurs to you. The writing is easy, it's the occurring that's hard.'

Tired of thinking, the writer tidies. She folds her sheets the way she saw on the Martha Stewart show and arranges fresh flowers in every room. In another life, the writer wants thin legs, three dogs, curly red hair, and to be a messy squirrel, but in this life none of the above applies. When the writer finishes tidying everything in sight, she eats afternoon tea, even though it's morning, and sets to work yet again.

The Reader

⟫ It's late, but I can't sleep. I don't want to go to school tomorrow. I dread seeing Dylan. I think I'm going to tell Ms Golightly that I've changed my mind about hanging out with her. This whole thing is really freaking me out. My fears toss and turn and refuse to leave. Mum sticks her head in, bearing tea and shortbread.

'I saw your light was on. I was thinking, Hon,' she says, 'about friends.'

'Mmm,' I reply, propping myself up in bed so I don't spill my drink.

'I reckon there are different sorts of friends for different occasions.'

'Such as?'

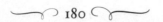

'Well, when I was at uni, my best friend was Carla. She was my wild friend, for dangerous fun and heavy drinking.'

'Mum!'

'I know, I know, it was a lifetime ago. Anyhow, after I married Dad and we had you, Carla and I didn't have much in common. She was still single and partying hard, so we just drifted apart.'

'What about now?'

'Let me see. Viv is my comfortable friend. We share things from our gardens, and we laugh a lot. She radiates kindness, and she's the least judge-mental person I know. Rowena is my intelligent friend, for books and philosophy. Maggy's my movie chum and an expert in clothing advice.'

'What about Freya?'

'Freya is my everything friend. But not everyone is lucky enough to have an everything friend. Annie is yours, maybe.'

'Yeah,' I say. 'I really miss her. Cheers, Mum, anyway. That was helpful.'

'Is that girl Dylan still giving you trouble?'

'Yeah, kinda. I'll tell you about it, but not now, okay?'

Mum wants to probe but, to her credit, she refrains. 'Sweet dreams,' she says, and tootles off to bed. I realise with amazement that she hasn't tried to improve me lately or suggest I do stuff her way.

It's a blooming miracle. I snuggle down and read a few pages of my book. I wish they'd hurry up and get to the ball. I can't wait to see what happens. I think Mirabella might be going to elope with Arlo.

CHAPTER
NEARLY THERE
AND A BIT

MISS HOPE, THE florist, was soaking her weary feet in a bucket of peppermint water, Mrs Blossom had a dreadful headache, the footmen were squabbling amongst themselves, and the peacocks had been relegated to a meadow far away because their squawking was driving everyone mad. It had been a week of scurrying madness, but now everything was in place for the grand ball to be held that very evening, the night of the full moon. Huge vases of pink chrysanthemums entwined with dainty fernery graced the entrance hall; the ballroom floor had been waxed and polished until it gleamed. The supper tables, spread with finest linen, were laden with a magnificent array of food: Mr Alfred's saffron buns and almond tarts, Mrs Blossom's spicy forcemeat balls dusted with nutmeg, chicken savouries, crab quenelles, caramel crepes, and marzipan mice. Posies of white roses decorated trays of glistening glasses which were waiting to be filled with ginger-fizz punch. Elda carefully placed a strawberry in each one, sighed, and looked down at her brown brogues. How she'd love to be a dancing duchess at the ball. Elda tried not to mind being a servant, and managed — most of the time. She was hoping scraps of gossip would filter down to the kitchen with the footmen as they delivered dirty glasses and platters to be washed. Rolf whistled as he wiped down the marble kitchen benches with hot soapy water, trying to drown out Mrs Blossom's whingeing and complaining.

'I never had a more difficult day in my entire life. My head is aching fair fit to burst. I do believe a bunch of trolls is doing a ju-ju dance in my noggin, it thumps so bad. As for supper, what a disaster! My pastry for them almond tarts is stodgy as a parson's lecture, and my forcemeat balls is saltier than mermaid's widdle. There will be complaints for certain. Mercy me, I should never have become a cook, but stuck to milk-maiding like my muvver said I ought have ... If you don't stop that bleedin' whistling, Rolf, I'll have your guts for sausage skins.'

In Mirabella's chambers, Glory was helping the princess dress for the ball. The last four days had been the longest in her life. Fear was her constant companion, accompanying her everywhere like a skull perched on her shoulder. However, nothing untoward had happened, unless you count Mrs Blossom's threatening to leave, which was apparently common on such occasions. Though Glory had not spoken of it, her friends knew how troubled she was, and had tried to comfort her.

'I don't believe in curses and witchery,' Rolf said. 'Such things are not rational and scientific. They are old wives' tales, designed to keep folk frightened. You must not let it scare you. Midnight will come and go, but nothing bad will happen, you'll see.'

Rolf believed his own reasoning, yet he was worried. He daren't burden Glory with his anxiety, but his hands trembled a little as he went about his chores.

'I fear there's truth in magic and spells, though I've never seen any magic with my own eyes. Perhaps if you don't believe in the curse it will not come true? If you don't give it no power over you.' Elda suggested.

'Thank you, Dear Friends.' Glory appreciated their kindness, but it did not lesson her rising terror.

These past days, Princess Mirabella had been kind and even-tempered towards Glory. She felt much fonder toward her maid since their time together in the rose garden. However, she did not known how to handle the matter of the curse. Realising the delicacy of the situation, the princess consulted her parents. After some deliberation, the king and queen advised her not to mention the curse but to ready herself for the forthcoming occasion and treat her chambermaid as usual. They knew no way around the problem, and their attention was focused on a flurry of protocols and preparations for the ball, the outcome of which would determine their own fate.

One afternoon, when her fear almost overcame her, Glory visited Miss Oleander. She saw through the window that the apothecary was busy tending a sick groomsman, so she didn't linger, but walked back and forth in the rose garden until her alarm subsided and she was calm enough to return to her duties. Mirabella did not mention her absence, and royal life continued as usual, the curse put aside amongst the petticoats and pearls.

'Are you sure my tiara is pinned securely and my hair is firmly fastened? It mustn't tumble down during the evening. Drat and dragons, my complexion looks as mottled as old cheese rind.'

'All is as it should be, truly,' Glory assured the princess, tucking a last curl into place. 'You look radiant. Your dress is exquisite, your jewels are dazzling, and your skin is smooth as milk.'

Glory glanced at the clock. It was seven o'clock, half an hour before the guests would arrive in their coaches and carriages. There would be music, merriment, and magnificence for many on this magical night, but not for her. Time had run out. Midnight was imminent. She was doomed.

The Reader

》 I wake with a vaguely sick feeling in my guts, shower, get dressed, thump around the kitchen, and shovel in a bowl of muesli.

'What's wrong, Petal?' Mum asks, but I can't tell her. I pin on my lucky blue glass dragonfly, throw a mandarin in my bag along with my ham salad roll, air-kiss Dad's photo on my way down the hall. I have to face the day. There's no escape.

THE WRITER

Some of the threads in her story are weaving together nicely, but others dangle in her brain like wet spaghetti. <u>Trust the Process</u>, the writer's sister suggests in an email. The writer prints <u>Trust the Process</u> in big letters on a big piece of cardboard and props it on her desk. It's the right wisdom to help guide her to the end of the book. Creativity usually triumphs, despite her worrying that it won't. Amongst what's for dinner, hair appointments, friends who pop in, walks, email, groceries, and a bit of telly, the story is worming its way out of her brain, out of the pile of notes on her desk and the dark fertile cosmos and onto the page.

CHAPTER WITH DRAMAS, DANCING AND DOUBTS

KING HAROLD, QUEEN Petronilla, and Princess Mirabella stood in stately attendance in the marble entry foyer as Arlo, in new red velvet livery and black hose, announced the arrivals. Mirabella kept a royal smile upon her face, but her heart sank as the procession of underwhelming guests was presented: fat counts, doddery dukes, and prattling princes who were far too young and rather spotty. William de Montague cut a fine figure, but the queen had warned Mirabella about his character: 'Don't waste your time considering him, Daughter; there is good reason why he's known as William the Bastard.'

'I am honoured to finally meet you, Princess Mirabella. I have long heard tell of your beauty and charm,' de Montague said, bowing low. 'Sadly, my brother, Bernard, is unable to attend this grand occasion, though he sends his most humble apologies,' de Montague lied, trying to forget the sight of his drooling brother handcuffed to his bed, making gutteral sounds.

'We're so sorry Prince Bernard is unable to join us this evening,' Queen Petronilla replied graciously. 'Please, enjoy your evening and pass along our kindest regards to your brother.'

'Whew, one less to consider. That gets rid of Bernard the Mad,' Mirabella mentally noted.

'Prince Swythyn of Alderly,' Arlo trumpeted, as the next guest approached. Poor Swythyn was trying so hard not to trip over his shoes that he bumped into the floral arrangement, spilling a puddle of water onto the marble floor. His poor, silly face reminded the princess of her childhood hamster.

'Charmed and delighted,' Mirabella curtsied. *If I*

have to cut off my ears and eat them, I shall not be marrying you, she thought to herself.

The next arrival was the Earl of Twickenham, a charming fellow whose reputation as a man who drank to excess was well-known.

'Honoured and thrilled,' Mirabella curtsied. *If I have to kill butterflies and boil babies, I shall not be marrying you.* Her smile was fake and frozen. The princess hoped her silent observations were not written upon her face for all to see.

The procession of guests began to thin. Princess Imogen swanned in next, accompanied by her mother, Queen Lila. Imogen was a vision splendid in a creation of frothy pink tulle, tiny rosebuds in her dark hair.

'Welcome, dear Cuz.' Imogen was the first person Mirabella was actually glad to see. As children, the two girls had often enjoyed gentle games and laughter together, one so dark and one so fair, as fetching as Snow White and Rose Red.

My toes are dreadfully pinched in these high-heeled slippers, Petronilla sighed silently. *What a long night it's going to be. Where, oh where, is King Gilbert? I call upon the fates: do not deny us the company of Prince Leonard and Prince Timothy. They're our only hope.*

The king stood regally, to all appearances the genial host, but his heart was heavy. He knew it was wrong to marry off his daughter in order to further his own ends. He wanted to be a good king, to rule with a firm hand, and had tried his best, he was sure he had. But perhaps he hadn't tried hard enough? For here he stood, like a stuffed parrot, at the mercy of the whims of others: his difficult daughter and the sketchy possibility of a husband who might not even eventuate.

'King Gilbert, Prince Timothy, and Prince Leonard, of the House of Ussher.' Arlo announced their arrival, then gave an extra loud blast on his trumpet. Queen Petronilla bestowed her most radiant smile, and the two kings shook hands mightily. They didn't know each other well, but had once hunted together and found each other good company. Mirabella gave the portly visitor a deep curtsey. His face showed intelligence and good cheer, but her real interest was in his oldest son, for, despite herself, the princess was curious about Prince Timothy. She curtsied once more and raised her eyes to greet the young man in front of her. The first thing she noticed was his physique. He was tall and burly, as powerful as a stallion, and his composure was steady. Mirabella was overcome by a most peculiar feeling. It was as if she'd met him long long ago, for he seemed as familiar to her as her own feet. The princess found this a heady mixture of divine and unwelcome. She regarded the prince without expression, and his clear blue eyes met her gaze steadily.

'Welcome.' Her voice came out louder than she wished, and her heart gave a small, unseemly lurch.

'Delighted to meet you. I've heard much about you,'

replied the prince, bowing low. He stepped briskly aside and his brother replaced him. Prince Leonard was indeed handsome, with fair curls and a winning smile, but the princess felt nothing special towards him.

When the late arrivals had entered the grand ballroom, the king, queen and princess followed. They took their places on the podium and the king gave a greeting.

'My dear wife, Queen Petronilla, and my lovely daughter, Princess Mirabella, and I welcome you. We bid you the happiest of evenings. Let the dancing begin.'

The band struck up a waltz and the royal couple took to the floor, setting the scene for others to follow. William of Montague lost no time in asking Mirabella to dance, but even as her body performed the necessary movements her thoughts were drawn to Prince Timothy. She couldn't help but notice that he'd beaten Swythyn of Alderly to partnering Princess Imogen in the dance.

He lacked warmth towards me. Obviously my reputation as a difficult person has preceded me, Mirabella thought sadly. *Imogen is both pretty and sweet-natured. I have no chance with him.*

As the evening progressed, the princess danced with every nobleman in the room except the one she wished for. William of Montague reminded her of a lizard, Swythyn of Alderly was a well-meaning simpleton, Thomas of Wychwood smelled peculiar, the Earl of Twickenham reeked of rum. Prince Leonard thought himself charming but had a braying laugh and spoke only of his own interests.

In the kitchen, Glory, Rolf, and Elda sat solemnly. Mrs Blossom had retired for the night with a willow bark brew and a bottle of brandy, and the footmen were all on duty in the supper room. Elda tried to cheer the mood with small talk, to no avail.

'I wonder how it's going? If Mirabella decides upon a husband, perhaps he won't agree to marry her. Everyone knows she's not the easiest of women, although she's been a lot nicer lately. I do believe your presence has softened her...'

Glory didn't reply, but sat glumly watching Rolf roll a walnut back and forth across the table. All the terrified girl could think about was the rising moon and the waning minutes left before the curse took hold. It did not seem real that these were to be her last hours alive. Perhaps it was just a cruel hoax, but if it were not...

'I'm going to stand in the shadows outside the ballroom and peek in. You can almost see what's happening if you stand on tiptoes. I did it when Mark of Pemberly were knighted. Shall we all go?' Elda suggested wistfully.

'I think not,' said Rolf, having glanced at Glory, who shook her head. 'You go ahead, Elda, and come back and tell us all about it.'

The kitchen was silent once Elda had gone, but

for the rolling sound of the walnut and the ticking of the clock. The waiting was unbearable.

'Come,' Rolf said suddenly. 'I want to show you something.' He grabbed Glory's hand and did not let go, leading her outside into the yard. The moon had risen and hung above them like a talisman. They did not speak, but walked together past the kitchen garden and the lily pond to the velvety lawn of the lower garden.

'Look,' said Rolf, pointing at the newly trimmed topiary trees which provided a veritable display of wonderment. A teacup, a twisted twirl, a peacock, a dachshund, and a mushroom all cast their doubles in shadow form, bright moonlight illuminating the spaces between. Without a word spoken, Rolf and Glory began running in and out and around the shapes, chasing each other like wild moonlight creatures. Finally, exhausted, they lay down on the grass together.

'Whatever happens tonight you must know—' Rolf began.

'Shhh,' Glory said urgently.

Rolf was puzzled, not expecting to be stopped so soon, even before he'd begun to declare himself.

'Listen, Rolf,' she urged, and the young man realised that Glory wished to halt him not because of any desire to cast off his declaration, but because an alarming noise was coming from behind the hedge.

'It sounds like a wounded animal. Perhaps it's a squirrel caught in a trap ...'

They leapt up and raced towards the ghastly retching sound.

'Look! It's Arabella!' The queen's dog ran hither and thither, gasping in great distress, stopping only to claw at her throat with front paws.

'We must catch her, Rolf!' The pair made chase but the frightened animal continued to dart in and out amongst the darkened foliage. Glory stumbled and made a futile grab.

'Do something Rolf! I fear she is dying.'

The young man sprinted, garnering his strength, and pounced on the terrified animal.

'This is most dreadful,' he exclaimed, moving from the darkness into a patch of moonlight. 'There's something stuck in her throat.'

'Hold her still. We must help her.'

The little dog wriggled wildly, but Rolf held tight.

'Open her jaws, open them wide, so we can see what is lodged there,' said Glory.

'Damn, she bit me!' How Rolf wished for another pair of hands! Keeping the squirming dog still at the same time as propping her small jaws apart was almost impossible. With great difficulty, he secured Arabella under one arm, using his other hand to keep the dog's mouth open.

'It's a chicken bone, stuck tight.'

Glory poked her finger in to dislodge the bone, to no avail. It was jammed so tightly she could not

budge it, and her task was made more difficult by the desperate nips of the poor frightened dog.

'Poking it from the front isn't working. Hold her still a little longer, Rolf. Perhaps I can hook it from behind — that is, if I can get my finger in.' Glory prayed for divine guidance, that she might save her canine friend. It took every ounce of her concentration to perform the delicate task. The dog quietened slightly, as if understanding help was being offered.

'There!' Glory waved the lethal object triumphantly, then threw it on the ground. Rolf picked it up and put it in his pocket, for safety. They sank back on the lawn, greatly relieved. Arabella licked Glory's fingers, then with a glad bark, she snuggled in beside them.

'I could not have borne to lose this naughty rascal. I have become very fond of her. So Rolf, as you were about to say...' Glory murmured, as she stroked the wee dog's head to calm it.

'I was about to say you are the most amazing girl, but there's something more important to say now, I think you'll agree?'

'Thank goodness that's over?' Glory felt light-headed and muddled in the aftermath of such excitement. Her heart was beating faster than usual; she wasn't sure if she was hot or cold, and she had no idea what he was getting at.

'No, you daft girl. Don't you see?' Rolf was almost yelling. 'You've saved a life!'

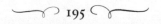

'But it was a *dog*. Surely that wouldn't count, would it?'

'Of course it would count. Dogs, and insects, and birds, and fish, and lizards are just as important as people. Every scientist knows this. Humankind is just one species amongst many. We think we're so important, but really all species are of equal value.'

Glory considered for a moment.

'I see what you mean. If only you're right, Rolf.'

She jumped up, taking his hand once more. 'Miss Oleander will confirm the veracity of your claim, if anyone can. We must go to her at once — that is, if you can bear to accompany this daft girl?'

'I would go just about anywhere, anytime, with you, Daft Girl, as I think you know.'

'Come on then, Daft Lad.'

Off they went, Arabella at their heels, hopeful that the dark spell had been broken.

THE WRITER

Today she's happy. She can see her way to the end. The writer realises it's mercurial, bordering on nut-bar, to veer from despair to joy so quickly, but, like it or lump it, this is the way she's wired. A peacock has to be a peacock, a giraffe has to be a giraffe. Some people are steady and calm, but the writer is more up-and-downish. Sometimes she's gloomy, sometimes she's joyous. Over-sensitive, prone to moodiness, happiest at home in her pyjamas, moodling around in her world of words.

As if to echo her mood, in a metaphoric swerve of meteorological aptness, the sun appears after a week of disappointing summer weather. For lunch, the writer eats a quesadilla oozing with cheese, then two nectarines. She brews Earl Grey in her favourite teapot, then wanders around inspecting her garden. How blessed she feels to live in this quiet place, in a land untouched by famine, flood, or war. Her pink tea roses are past their best, the cacti look great, the zucchini need picking—she'll grate them into pancakes, with

mint and feta, for dinner tonight. The blue
mosaic steps could do with a sweep, and maybe
she'll plant some more marigolds. But first,
she has a book to finish.

The Reader

》 Dylan wasn't in Lit, which was my first class today,
but I didn't have time to stress about it because Mr J
had arranged for a mad Italian writer of teen fiction
to run a Creative Writing workshop. First, we had to
give ourselves new names, to get us in an inventive
mood. I chose Miss Teacup, Kaz was Two-Minute-
Noodle Girl, Melanie was Vampire 13. Next, the guy
asked for every word we could possibly think of that
had anything to do with the beach. He scribbled
dozens of them on the board: all the obvious ones,
like hot, splash, waves, water, sun, ocean, sand, and
ice-cream, and lots of random ones as well. Then
we had to write a piece about the beach, but we
weren't allowed to use any of the words. You couldn't
put substitutes, either—like you couldn't put H_2O
instead of water. We grumbled like mad because

he'd tricked us, but it was actually challenging and fun. All in all, a good morning, because in Biology we discussed Darwin and the Origin of the Species, which was interesting. I was hanging round in the hall with Kaz before lunch when Toby tapped me on the shoulder. I tried not to remember how bad kissing him had been.

'Hey, Nova. I was in the office handing in my late pass and they sent me to find you and give you a message. You have to go to Ms Golightly, right now.'

'Why?'

'I dunno. You're probably totally in the shit about something...'

'Yeah, right. Okay, I'll check it out.'

The door of the counsellor's office is half-closed so I knock and wait, uncertain.

'Come in, if you're Nova,' Ms G calls, and ushers me in. She's wearing blue today: blue pumps, blue leggings, and a bright blue-and-gold tunic made of sari material. Continuing the Indian theme, she's sporting blue bling earrings and lots of tiny bangles. Her face isn't all Bollywood smiley, though. She's in serious mode. Dylan is there, too, her face blotchy with crying.

'Dylan's got a few things she'd like to say to you; right, Dylan?'

'Yeah.' She tosses her long blonde hair out of her

face and blows her nose loudly. I can tell she has to make a real effort to pull herself together, but she does. 'I'm sorry, Nova. I shouldn't have been so mean, and I'm really sorry for breaking in and trying to rip you off. I've been really messy lately, because of Dad and a whole lot of other stuff, actually, but . . . I want to get myself together, I really do.'

'Okay,' I reply. It sounds a bit lame, but *I forgive you* would sound even dumber. I can't even explain why, but I do want to give her another chance.

'Will you still do the hanging-out thing with me?' Dylan asks. 'Ms G thinks it would be a good idea, if you're up for it.'

'All right, if you really mean it. I don't want any more nasty surprises.'

'Totally.'

After what seemed like a clumsy silence, Ms G takes charge.

'It's your turn to choose the play-date this time, Nova. Sorry, that sounds a bit juvenile, but "activity" sounds too sensible. Remember, it has to be fun; something you really enjoy.'

I have a think. 'Well, I'd like to have someone to go to town with. We could go to Bead Bazaar, check out some vintage stores, just hang out.'

'You up for that, Dylan?'

'Sure. I have netball on Mondays, but any other afternoon is good.'

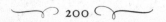

So, after school on Thursday, Dylan and I took the bus to the city. It felt awkward between us, at first.

'So, what's the plan?' Dylan asked, when we arrived at the bus station.

'I don't really have a plan; I just usually wander around. Are you hungry?'

'Always. I know a good sushi place. Want to check it out?'

When Dylan is happy, she looks lovely. Fuelled by an eight-pack of salmon sushi and some weirdly tasty green bubble tea, we made our way to Vintage Heaven, my favourite shop. It's chokka with goodies: furniture, crockery, old postcards, fabrics, toys, sewing items, and clothes from the fifties through to the eighties. The owner wears vampire lippie, and today her fake plaits were gathered up into a swirly concoction topped with a red felt hat. She was engrossed in a magazine and didn't seem to mind if we tried stuff on. Dylan looked neat in an old blue frock and lace elbow-length gloves, although they kind of clashed with her school shoes. I draped myself in a black antique shawl with long tassels and Spanish embroidery of a bird and roses. In its slinky loveliness, I was a summer princess, just like Mirabella.

Next, we mooched on down to Bead Bazaar.

'I've got money,' Dylan said. 'My parents came

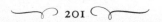

home last night and gave me the pocket money they owed me. We could make bracelets.'

'How *is* your father doing?' I asked, as we threaded tiny blue beads, sparkly crystals, green marbled ovals, and red orbs.

'A lot better, actually. The new treatment's helped a lot, and the doctor is pretty happy with his progress. Damn, these little blue babies are slippery...'

The best thing of all happened on our way home. When we got off the bus, Dylan said, seeing it was such a nice evening, she'd walk me home. Outside the library, two hunky-looking guys were sitting in a tree. One of them was playing the ukulele. I would have just strolled shyly past, but Dylan wandered over and called up to them.

'Cool ukulele. What sort is it?'

They climbed down and started chatting, so we sat with them and talked for ages. The quiet one with dark hair and glasses was Sebastian; the droll blond was Ned. They took our phone numbers. Brilliant!

'Which one do you like?' I asked Dylan when we finally peeled off.

'Both of them!'

'Me too!' We fell about laughing. Interesting to see who calls who—that is, if they do call. Lap of the gods, we decided.

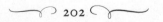

Now I'm sitting on my bed, painting my toenails a creamy coffee colour, going over everything and savouring it. It was the best afternoon I've ever had.

THE WRITER

No, that's too easy, too cheesy...

The Reader

》 Dylan wasn't at school this morning, but I didn't have time to worry about it because we had a Creative Writing workshop. We started by giving the person next to us a new name. I called Kaz Miss Teacup, she chose Vampire 13 for Melanie, and Mel christened me Two-Minute-Noodle Girl. Then we brainstormed words with a connection to beaches. The board was covered with them; all the obvious ones and lots of random ones as well. Our assignment was to write about the beach, not using any of the words. Afterwards, I was hanging round in the hall when Nigel Brown tapped me on the shoulder.

'Dragon Lady in the office sent me to find you. You have to go to Ms Golightly, at once.'

'Why?'

'I dunno. She probably wants to give you the Nobel Peace Prize...'

'Yeah, right. Okay, I'll check it out.'

The door was shut so I knocked and waited.

Ms G opened the door immediately and ushered me in. She was wearing a blue dress made from sari material, and blue bling earrings. Her face wasn't Bollywood smiley, though. She looked awfully serious.

'Sit down, Nova.' Ms G cleared her throat. I was starting to have a really bad feeling about this.

'I'm so sorry to have to tell you this, but I wanted you to hear it from me before it went around the school. I feel responsible for you because I've helped you get involved in something that couldn't have been predicted. Something awful has happened to Dylan.'

'What?' I didn't want her to continue.

'She visited you last night, right?'

'Yes, but how did you know?'

'The housekeeper who was looking after her told the police.'

'The police?' My voice was a strangled croak.

'When Dylan got home, she told the house-keeper where she'd been. She was pretty hysterical, apparently. The woman couldn't get her to settle down. Dylan took off into the night, so the police were called in to help find her.'

'And...'

'Her body was found at 6 a.m. this morning, in Kings Park, by a jogger.'

'She's dead?'

It couldn't be true. If I shut my eyes and opened them again she'd be sitting in the bean-bag, long blonde hair hanging down over her eyes, picking at that scaly skin around her fingernails.

Ms G nodded, holding back tears, then continued.

'There's to be an investigation, to rule out foul play, but it looks as if she took her own life.'

'How?'

'A mixture of pills and alcohol, they think. They've ordered a forensic report. It's best if you keep these details to yourself, Nova. Talk to your mother and father about it, of course, but beyond that the police want to keep the specifics under wraps, to protect her family. As you can imagine, this is the most horrific thing for her parents to face.'

I wanted to scream or throw something. I wanted to rip that head off Ms G's stupid little statue that promised goodness and purity. What a goddamn lie.

THE WRITER

Too harsh, too sudden, too grim...

The Reader

〉 I really didn't want to face today. Dylan wasn't in Lit this morning, but I didn't stress about it because we had a Creative Writing workshop. Afterwards, I was hanging round in the hall when Kaz tapped me on the shoulder.

'Hey, Nova. You have to go see Ms Golightly, right now.'

'Why?'

'Don't ask me, Babe.'

'Okay, I'll check it out.'

The door was open, so I went in. Ms G wore a blue-and-gold dress made of sari material, and jangly bangles. Dylan was there, too, her face blotchy from crying.

'Thanks for coming, Nova. Dylan's got a few things she'd like to say to you; right, Dylan?'

'Yeah.' She tossed her hair out of her face and blew her nose loudly. 'I'm sorry I broke in and tried to steal your stuff. I've been really messy lately, but I want to get myself together, I really do.'

'Okay,' I replied.

Dylan looked about as cheerful as if she'd just watched someone feed kittens to a pit-bull.

'The thing is, Ms G really wants us to do the hanging-out thing, but I'm just...I'm not up for it. It's not personal. I enjoyed it when we made cards, but I need to sort some things out for myself and I don't want any pressure...'

'Fine,' I mumbled, even though it didn't feel fine. It might not seem personal to Dylan but it is to me.

'Right,' said Ms G briskly. 'See you at your next session, Dylan. Have a good week. Nova, can you stick around?'

'Sure.'

'No hard feelings?' asked Dylan.

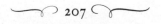

I couldn't even be bothered answering her. I just gave a limp wave as she left.

Ms G sat me down and dug a packet of cashews out of her desk drawer.

'Want some?'

'Nah, not really.'

'So, how are you feeling?'

'I feel pretty crap and I don't particularly want to talk about it, to be honest.'

'Fair enough. I feel pretty crap about what's happened, too, for the record. I have to respect Dylan's choices, though.'

'What would Kuan Yin say?' I asked. Maybe the little ivory statue has some wisdom, because I sure don't.

'She's all about compassion and kindness. Maybe those qualities would be helpful to you right now, as you struggle with your feelings of rejection. It may sound far-fetched, but imagine holding yourself in kind arms, and Dylan, too. She's really struggling, poor kid. Even stretch it as far as your dumb counsellor, who tried to organise something good that turned out badly.'

'Sounds like a plan,' I replied. I wasn't sure I could do what she suggested, but I could try.

'If it's any consolation, my boyfriend just ditched me.' Ms G took a handful of cashews and screwed up her face in an exaggerated gesture of woe.

'Really?'

'Yeah. I thought he was The One, but apparently he thinks a red-headed artist called Tania is The One.'

'What a scumbag.'

'He sort of is, but he's also human. Hey, why am I defending him? I have to hate him a bit first, then I'll take my own advice and get the kindness flowing.' Ms G grinned. 'Okay, kiddo. You'd better get back to class. Come and see me any time you want. I'll be here; me, and Kuan Yin, and maybe some chocolate.'

'Cheers,' I said, and scooted.

In Media, Dylan ignored me. I was actually glad. If we weren't going to be friends, why pretend? It wasn't the most peaceful afternoon inside my brain. One minute I was all hurt and the next minute I was thinking, *Well, who needs her? She has crap taste in music, for starters. Her faves are a wanker called DJ Earwax and bands with stupid names like Bark Psychosis.*

On the way home after school, wandering past the library, I saw the oddest thing. A guy was sitting in that big oak tree, playing a ukulele. With his dark hair and glasses he looked a bit like Jermaine from Flight of the Conchords, but younger, more like my age. His mobile phone fell down beside me so I picked it up and handed it to him after he slid down.

'Thanks.'

'Is it broken?'

'Doesn't seem to be.'

We both stood there awkwardly.

'See ya,' I said, and wandered off. If my life was a movie, he would have asked for my phone number. I'd have given it to him. He'd have called me and become the love of my life. But my life isn't a movie, and he didn't.

When I got home Mum was in the kitchen, putting away a pile of fancy groceries.

'Your father's luggage still hasn't turned up; can you believe it? We just got off the phone and, guess what, he's coming home early. Tomorrow, in fact.'

'Cool.'

She heard the flatness in my voice.

'What's wrong, Nova?'

I almost pretended nothing was wrong, but I decided I could do with a mama chat. I made a honey sandwich, and told her the whole Dylan saga.

'I'm bloody pissed off with her...' I said, and then I started to cry.

Mum's great. She let me have a good old boo-hoo, then gave me a hug and one of her touchy-feely talks.

'*Don't let anyone bring you low enough to hate them*. I can't remember who said that, but it was one of the bigs: Gandhi or Martin Luther King. There's just no point wasting your energy hating Dylan.

Friendships happen if they're meant to, and they don't if they aren't. You have to trust that everything is rolling the way it's meant to, even when it feels otherwise.'

'Do you really think so?'

'I do. Same with buying houses. They go to the right people. If it's meant to be, it will be. The trick is letting go and trusting the next bit. Easy to say and hard to do, I know, but I believe in it. *Trust emergence*, as they say.'

'*Trust in Allah but tether your camel*,' I responded. Mum and I used to do this all the time, share the nutty one-liners we came across. Our best one so far was: *People should follow their dreams, except the one where they're naked on the pavement.*

Mum giggled. 'I saw a goodie, today, on a chalk-board outside a café. *My favourite drink is a cocktail of whisky and carrot juice. It gets you really really drunk, but you can see for miles.* God, it will be good to see your father. I've really missed him, haven't you?'

CHAPTER MIDNIGHT

M ISS OLEANDER'S ONLY ornament was a brooch, a star of rubies. She wore a simple robe of grey linen, and her hair tumbled loose. Despite bare feet and lack of formality, the apothecary radiated great power — invisible but commanding. She put down her bowl when Glory entered with Arabella in her arms.

'I was expecting you. Is it the little one? Where is she wounded? Would you care for some of this walnut bread with pears in sweet wine while I attend to her?'

'How did you know we were coming?' Glory asked, puzzled.

'Let us not waste time with trivialities,' Miss Oleander replied, her dark eyes glittering.

'Indeed,' Rolf burst in. 'The curse, is it broken?'

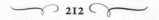

'It is.'

'Are you sure?'

'I am sure.'

There followed a shared silence, a vast pleasurable basking in stillness loud with joy

'I *would* like some of that food,' Glory said, after a while, suddenly realising she was hungry. She hadn't eaten for days; not properly, anyway.

'Of course, My Dear, of course. I think we might celebrate with a thimble of plum brandy.'

When Rolf and Glory left, Miss Oleander sat alone and sombre. She'd made light of it in order not to frighten her two young friends but Glory's escape had been narrow. Death had been near. The apothecary lit seven white candles and chanted an ancient blessing, offering thanks for the benevolent events of the full moon.

Mirabella wished the night was over, but it was only supper time. Her tiara felt a bit wobbly and so did she, having endured William of Montague's clammy hands, Thomas of Wychwood's musty odour, and Swythyn of Alderly's valiant attempts to put words into a coherent sentence. She was further discomforted by the fact that Prince Leonard had obviously only asked her to dance because King Gilbert nudged him into it, and that Prince Timothy had not asked her to dance at all.

She'd seen the tall, striking prince talking animatedly to Imogen during the first dance. Next, he'd dutifully waltzed with Queen Petronilla, but since then she hadn't seen him on the dance floor or, in fact, anywhere at all.

When supper was announced, King Harold took his daughter's arm and led her to an alcove where there was a little table and several gilded French chairs.

'Would you like something to drink, My Dear?'

'Thank you, Papa.' The king wandered off, leaving Mirabella alone, but not for long.

'Hello, Peach Pie.'

Mirabella looked up to see the cheeky face of her cousin Imogen.

'*Très horrible, n'est ce pas?*'

'Really? It seemed you were enjoying yourself with Prince Timothy.' Mirabella knew she sounded snide, but she couldn't muster the strength to be pleasant.

'He's all right, I suppose, though he spoke only of falconry. I've no interest in that most ancient of field sports, although I now know the difference between a broad wing and a long wing, should you care to hear.'

'Is he a good dancer?'

'He's strong, and leads a girl manfully, unlike that juggins Swythyn, whose steerage lacks conviction. Why, Cuz, such an interest in the prince?'

Mirabella was spared replying by the return of King Harold, bearing ginger-fizz punch. He kissed

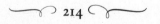

his niece, promised to arrange some supper for the pair, then went to greet his old friend Duke Tarquin, who'd made a late arrival due to an encounter with a wayward bear. The princesses discussed the lack of merits of the men at the ball.

'They all seem lacklustre, but perhaps that is because my heart is taken by another,' Imogen confessed.

'Do tell me about this man who has claimed your heart. I'm most keen to hear of it.'

Arlo arrived with a platter of dainties, but Mirabella waved him away without even a thank you, keen to hear about her cousin's paramour.

'Thomas Fitzgerald, Twenty-ninth Knight of Glin. He's ill with influenza this evening, so he was unable to attend the ball. My parents are not keen on our union, for he is rather a lot older than me, but I shall not give up until I am the wife of his house and the mistress of his bed. So, is Prince Timothy the man of *your* dreams, then?' Imogen teased. 'I notice you search the ballroom with your eyes as if you've lost your most precious earring, yet both your ears have their jewels intact . . .'

'Balderdash!'

Mirabella had been doing exactly that; however, the prince was nowhere to be seen, and she could not admit, even to herself, the effect he'd had upon her. She licked her fingers. 'Here, if you don't want this delicious saffron bun, I shall eat it myself.'

At that moment, Queen Petronilla bustled up.

'Where is the king? There's been an incident involving Arabella...'

'Is she all right, Mama?' Mirabella knew how her mother adored the little dog.

'It seems so. Rolf, the kitchen boy, has brought news. I must hasten to the apothecary, to see my darling with my own eyes. If you see your father, let him know what has occurred and where I am.'

The queen rushed away, Imogen drifted off to find more food, and Mirabella, seeing no sign of the man who'd made such an impression, decided to do the unthinkable and sneak away to bed. She gave the supper crowd a last fleeting glance, then made her way slowly through the empty ballroom. Two footmen stood in the doorway, stiff as posts. Mirabella lifted her head like a haughty swan, pretending she felt royal rather than ragged and miserable. In the entrance hall, silver candelabras dripped waterfalls of wax, as if to demonstrate that the promise of a bright evening was now dribbling away. Even the elaborate floral arrangements seemed to mock Mirabella, their extravagant beauty but a flimsy show. As the princess began her weary way up the staircase, she met Arlo coming down. Mirabella nodded, intending to walk straight past him, but the page bowed low and spoke. In his new outfit, he felt himself to be looking his best.

'Surely you are not leaving so early? You're not unwell, Your Highness?'

Mirabella found his enquiry impertinent, yet could not think how best to answer him. Thoughts and feelings were wandering around her head in strange unruly paths; the events of the evening had quite undone her. Leaning close, she whispered in his ear.

'There are some things a lady must never tell.'

Arlo had spent the evening drinking ale with the other footmen. It was strictly forbidden, but they always did it on such occasions between their duties, to alleviate the boredom. Arlo misinterpreted Mirabella's words as flirtatiousness and, in a random fit of beery madness, he drew the princess to him in a passionate embrace.

'What on earth are you thinking?'

Even though she'd entertained a few unsuitable notions about this young peacock, Mirabella was furious. She pulled away, incensed. Arlo, appalled by the rebuttal and his breech of protocol, hurried past, stumbling as he did so. The princess looked back and saw with dismay that Prince Timothy, who was standing in the foyer, had witnessed the entire event. Arlo slunk past him like a wet fox. Mirabella wanted to run down and explain everything, but the stern expression on the prince's face halted her. She made her way forlornly to her chambers. Her chambermaid should have been waiting to help her undress, but Glory was not there. Mirabella couldn't even be bothered being vexed. She took off her tiara and her jewellery, her dancing shoes and her beautiful dress, threw them on the floor, hopped into her four-poster bed in her satin underwear, and wept herself to sleep.

When the princess woke after a night of savage dreams, Glory had tidied the room and bought a tray of fruits and pastries.

'Good morning, Your Highness.'

Suddenly, Mirabella remembered the importance of the previous midnight hour.

'Sit!' she commanded, and over breakfast she heard all about the events of the previous evening.

'How wonderful to hear of it,' Mirabella said with genuine relief.

'Oh, my goodness!' Glory leapt to her feet and curtsied low. 'I'm so very sorry, Your Highness!'

'Why?'

'I am not myself! I completely forgot. King Gilbert and his sons stayed at the palace last night, and I'm to give you this...'

Glory slid a small green envelope with a falcon crest from the pocket of her apron and handed it to Mirabella.

'Thank you. You may return my tray now.' The princess wished to read the note in privacy.

Would you care to come riding this morning? It was signed with the letter T.

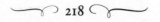

When Glory arrived in the kitchen, Mrs Blossom had just made a pot of tea strong enough for a mouse to trot on. She gathered Glory to her massive bosom with joy.

'Plum diddly! Dear Child, you are saved!'

Elda was humming, Rolf was whistling...

THE WRITER

Rolf was whistling, and then what the hell happened? Anyway, he's always whistling. He needs to be doing something else. The writer reaches into her brain, seeking an alternative activity to indicate Rolf's happiness, but finds only emptiness. Writing the end of this book is the hardest part of all. The blue pieces don't seem to fit, and she hasn't got enough red pieces. The whole quilt suddenly seems to have been a complete waste of time. She wanted her book to have, as Dickens said, comedy and tragedy mixed together like streaky bacon, but fears it might be turning out like a bad pie with a soggy crust and dodgy filling. The writer swears she will never write another book again. She wanders from the fridge to the garden, eating dark chocolate, and pulling up dandelions. A more famous writer said that near the end of a novel everything fits into your book: the three-legged dog you see in the park, the particular piece of music you hear in a café, the wet rose in the evening light. It's as if the world is channelling the story straight to your fingers, the famous one said. How delightful this sounds, the writer says bitterly, but it is poppycock-a word she aimed to put in her book but hasn't been able to find the right place for. However, she can't give up. Mirabella has to resolve her love stuff, and Glory has a trip to make, and...

The Reader

》 Last night, I dreamt about the boy in the tree. His name was Sebastian. In real life, I'd rather he were called Ned. Anyhow, in my dream I kissed him. It was a light, elegant kiss. He tasted like seaweed and honey.

THE LOVEY-
DOVEY CHAPTER

'OF COURSE I will come riding with you!' Mirabella yelled as she jumped out of bed. 'Where's Glory when I need her?' She rang her bell loudly, and Arlo skulked in. He'd been lurking in the hall, trying to muster the courage to apologise before he lost his job or his head.

'Last night *did not happen*. That's that,' Mirabella said in a voice of steel.

Arlo nodded with relief.

'Now, deliver this message to Prince Timothy. You'll probably find him in the breakfast room, dining with my parents. Tell him the princess is keen to ride, and will meet him at the stables. Hurry!'

The princess donned her riding outfit, spat on her boots, wiped them with her sleeve, tucked her hair into a French roll, pinched her cheeks to make them pinker, smudged rose balm on her lips, and made her way to the stables. The prince wasn't there when she arrived, but Mirabella didn't worry unduly; not at first. She inspected Oak's hooves and chatted to the groomsmen about saddlery, but as time passed she became impatient. Surely the prince should be here by now? Was he playing a cruel trick on her? Perhaps Arlo didn't deliver her note safely? Mirabella's thoughts became angrier as time passed. It seemed to her that the stable boy and the head groomsman were whispering about her as they shovelled straw. Perhaps the prince wanted to humiliate her, because he had seen what happened on the stairs? How could he be such a cruel person? Finally, the princess lost patience all together. *I'll ride without him*, she decided. So, Mirabella mounted Oak, gave him a good strong kick, and galloped off.

She rode hard, over hill and down dale. Her favourite ride was across the pasture beyond the castle, over a hedge or two, then through the woods, returning slowly along the bank of the stream. She usually stopped to rest when she came out of the woods, where the stream began, at the site of a ruined mill. Her thoughts were wild and muddled, so the princess gave Oak his rein, and her trusty steed traversed their usual path at tremendous gait. Both horse and rider were hot and bothered by the time they arrived at the glade.

Prince Timothy was a clever man. He knew many things beside the intricacies of falconry. He knew it was time he took a wife. His father, King Gilbert, was unwell, and soon he himself would inherit the crown. Running a kingdom was no job for a lonely bachelor. Princess Mirabella was known to be difficult and unwilling to marry, but her feisty reputation intrigued the prince, who enjoyed a challenge. When he set eyes on Mirabella, he was dazzled — not only by her beauty, but by an indescribable essence that other women lacked. Heart and mind concurred. *I shall risk all*, he decided, *and court her*. The prince knew that, with women as with falcons, an obvious move is not the best one. He'd planned to ask Mirabella for the last dance, to make her wait a little for his attentions, if you like. However, her sulky decision to leave the ball early had foiled that particular manoeuvre, so he'd followed her from the ballroom, desiring to speak with her. The prince had seen what happened on the stairs, but it hadn't deterred him. He spent the early hours in the East Gallery, drinking strong mead and gambling on cards with Prince Leonard, King Gilbert, Duke Tarquin, and King Harold.

'I want to marry your daughter,' he'd told King Harold, just before they retired, seeing no point beating about the bush. Prince Leonard nearly choked on his drink, Tarquin raised a quizzical eyebrow, and his father kicked him under the table to advise caution, but King Harold was delighted, both by Timothy's honesty and his intent.

'There's nothing I would like more, but I'm afraid Mirabella is a very stubborn young woman. She's determined not to be married off like a sack of potatoes, as she sees it.'

'So I've heard. However, if I can persuade your daughter to be my wife, you have no objection?'

The king reiterated his support.

'Objection? Hardly! I would be honoured and thrilled, good fellow.'

'I hear the princess is a keen horsewoman and rides each morning. Where does she usually go?'

So it was that, when Mirabella arrived in the glade, she was greeted by the sight of Prince Timothy lying under a tree, grinning. Mirabella dismounted and tethered her horse. She was incredibly pleased to see the prince, and she also wanted to give him a right royal blasting. Instead, she lay down on the soft grass beside him. She didn't ask why he hadn't met her in the stable, she just returned his smile with a wink. The pair lay on their backs, watching clouds scuttle into fantastic shapes.

'So, would you care to hear about my falcons?' the prince asked languidly, when he finally spoke.

'Not really. At least, not right now. Perhaps some other time. My cousin Imogen has warned me that once you get onto that topic it is hard to interest you in any other.'

'You really are the most disagreeable, most

compelling woman. but you don't scare me. I was raised on tales of my ancestors. Queen Olive of Norwich, for example, mother of Marquis De La Pasture. When her son was beheaded by the enemy, she drank his blood to rally the troops. As you can see, I come from people of extremely strong mettle.'

'Gadzooks!' said the princess. She wasn't exactly sure what the word meant, but she'd always wanted to use it and now seemed to be the right occasion.

'So,' the prince continued, unfazed by her odd expression. 'Do you fancy your pretty pageboy, then?'

'Don't be ridiculous. Not in the least,' Mirabella said indignantly. 'I can explain —'

'No need. I'd rather hear what can you do that is useful. Can you dig a hole, bake a loaf, plant a flower? Can you deliver a child or milk a cow? Or are you only interested in your own wellbeing?'

'I beg your pardon?'

'I seek a wife. Beauty does not interest me, although you are very lovely, I will admit. But beauty fades, and life is longer than that. I need a queen who will help me run my kingdom in new ways, to create a land where all are fairly treated. She'll need to share the power and the duties of the state, and be familiar with the ways of the world.'

'I could learn to do those things, I'm sure. I don't think you will find many princesses who are already skilled at them. What I *am* passionate about is horses.

I want to breed them, one day. I admit I've not yet learnt to be very interested in people. My horizons will need expanding, in that regard. I could probably get interested in falcons, if the right man taught me about them.'

'I admire your honesty,' replied the prince. 'I have never met a maiden with such insight into her own strengths and weaknesses.'

'In that case,' said Mirabella, who was another person who didn't believe in beating about the bush, 'do you want to marry me?'

The prince took his time replying. He scratched his head solemnly, as if having to think hard about his answer. Then he picked a blade of shivery grass and gently tickled Mirabella's ankle with it.

'Actually,' he told her, 'I do.'

The Reader

〉 Mum says she doesn't feel like Indian food tonight. Dad suggests a new place called Quesadilla, that serves modern Mexican food. It's delicious: guacamole, blue corn chips, mango and coriander salsa, grilled tortilla with chicken and cheese in the middle, which is what quesadilla are, I learn.

'We have news,' Mum announces. They stare at me like two happy chipmunks.

'What?'

'Dad's been offered a year's contract in Chile. We want to go.'

'Just you two?' I say, my stomach sinking. Everyone has a boarding school fantasy, but I'm not keen on experiencing it for real.

'No, Dafty, all of us. It'll be a major adventure. If you want to, that is?'

'Yeah, of course I do! But what about school? I mean, I can't just leave . . .'

'There's an International school. You'll have to learn Spanish, though. It's a biggie so we'll understand if you need time to think about it, or you don't want to.'

I take a deep breath. My tummy is trembly, my head is spinning, but I'm ready for an adventure.

'*Hola! Buenos Dias!* Enchilada!' I blurt. 'What's not to like?'

We're all laughing, and I think *Maybe I can get over Dylan*. Not everyone has to like me. Things won't always turn out just the way I want. No doubt the new school will be a bit daunting, but right now everything feels exactly as it is supposed to. All my ducks are in a row and, even though I know they won't stay there for long, I'm savouring it, being happy, right here and right now, in this restaurant, with my mum and dad and a dob of salsa on my chin.

THE WEDDING CHAPTER

PRINCE TIMOTHY GAVE Mirabella a gold ring set with an emerald the size of a quail's egg, which he happened to have in his pocket. Then he returned to his kingdom to make the necessary arrangements.

That evening, in bed by candlelight, Queen Petronilla and King Harold shared figs, cheddar cheese, and a bottle of claret.

'I pledge to help you more and growl at you less,' Petronilla murmured, after her second goblet.

'And I, for my part, aim to be a worthwhile king and husband. I've been much inspired by hearing Prince Timothy speak of his dreams for the kingdom. He wishes to create equality for all: valets and footmen, grooms and cooks, seamstresses and maids. His vision is for a prosperous land where all may live in harmony.'

'What an extraordinary idea!'

'Perhaps, but one worthy of the highest consideration, don't you agree, My Petal?' The king sighed and continued. 'I shall miss her, you know, our difficult daughter...'

'I will, too, but birds must leave the nest eventually. I think we'll find ways to amuse ourselves, do you not?' the queen replied, snuggling down into the royal bed.

The king couldn't believe his luck. His daughter marrying a good man of her own choice, and the queen had offered him some rumpty-tumpty!

The wedding took place on a new moon. Mirabella wore a white silk gown with a beaded bodice, a

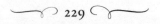

cascading skirt, and a train of chiffon embroidered with gold thread. She held a bouquet of red rosebuds. A small chamber quartet heralded the bride down the aisle, where Prince Timothy stood, proud in white breeches and a red satin waistcoat. The queen dabbed her eyes, and the king gave a sigh of relief. The prince and princess exchanged vows under an orange blossom bower; servants and noblemen alike threw confetti of delphinium petals. Then the merriment began. Scented candles lit the way for the bridal waltz, and jasmine cast sexy fragrance into the corners of the night. When the musicians took a break, an accordion player in a black hat played gypsy tunes, wild and free. Dirk, the beekeeper, became jug-bitten on blood-and-thunder, a mixture of port wine and brandy. He grabbed Mrs Blossom and called her My Beautiful Mountain. 'You're drunk as a wheelbarrow!' Mrs Blossom gasped, but rested in his embrace, bold as a zinnia. Elda got tiddly on shandy gaff, a blend of ale and ginger beer. She took an unruly giggling fit, and had to be given a peppermint by Arlo to calm her down.

As for the food! You've never seen anything like it! Trout with dill, pigeon baked with rum and raisins, a goose with a duck baked inside it and a tiny quail baked inside that, chickens stuffed with sausage and chestnuts, vegetables roasted with rosemary and honey, creamy custards flavoured with nutmeg, pyramids of fruit, and crystal jellies perfumed with rosewater, all washed down with elderflower champagne and finest ale. The wedding gifts included one hundred and seven pairs of sheets, one hundred and fifty tablecloths, one hundred doves, three gilded carriages, two fine black horses, a host of hideous ornaments and snuff boxes, and a partridge in a pear tree. Tarquin gave them a country estate, Swythyn of Alderly sent a gift of three pigs. Two of the groomsmen had to be disciplined by the head butler, due to drunkenness that led to food throwing, and a jolly good time was had by all.

When the bridal couple had departed for their honeymoon, the King and Queen went wearily to bed. Arabella dozed happily on a satin cushion besides them. Most of the guests had left in their carriages but a few late-night revellers continued to quaff ale, sharing bawdy tales and the last of the sweetmeats.

Rolf and Glory snuck away to the stargazing turret. The sky was a milky muddle of stars; the air was warm upon their skin. The pair sat together peacefully, enjoying the balmy night. Rolf took Glory's hand.

'Our wedding shall be a much simpler affair,' he said quietly.

'Yes.' Glory smiled and squeezed his hand. And so it was agreed, without fuss or fanfare. Each knew they were meant to be together, there was no need for folderol. Life was a glorious messy mystery that tumbled all around, abundant with ducks and herbs, moons and horses, walnuts and libraries and slippers. It had its own weathers and ways. It couldn't be bought or sold, bartered or fully understood, and for Rolf and Glory there was no doubt that they would spend the entirety of it together. The deal was sealed between them, not with a fancy ring but with the sweetest of kisses, as the darkness faded and the new light dawned.

A few days later, the queen offered Glory the chance to visit her mother. Elda and Mrs Blossom took a break from shelling peas and came into the yard to wave goodbye. Rolf produced two conker nuts, a rock embedded with a fossilised fern, and a wooden top, to give her brothers. Miss Oleander smiled and handed Glory more gifts: some elderflower cordial, a tincture for Rosamund, and a leather medicine box containing willow bark for headaches, calendula for bruising, tansy for fevers, and peppermint for indigestion.

'You won't need that with my food,' bellowed Mrs Blossom, thrusting a box of victuals into Mr Hobb's arms for them to share on the journey.

Glory departed with great elation, but the road moved slow as the carriage bounced and bumped its way along. She wanted to be there and back again, all in the same moment. She missed Rolf already, but she couldn't wait to see her dear ones and tell them all that had happened at the palace.

Jakob and Ptolemy were catching frogs for the pure pleasure of letting them go. They were good-natured lads and easy to amuse. Gerard, the carpenter, had given them some wood scraps and a handful of nails. How they loved to hammer. What manner of strange boats they produced, and a creature like a square elephant with leaves for ears. Their mother had tried not to let them see how much she missed Glory, amusing them with tiddlywinks and dominoes, songs and riddles. The daytime was not so bad, for she was fearsome busy, but at night her heart ached for news of her daughter.

That autumn afternoon, as she made barley soup, Rosamund heard a cacophony of shouting, and rushed out to see what the commotion was. She was greeted by the sight of Mr Hobbs helping Glory down, while Jakob and Ptolemy yelled and leapt about with glee.

'Oh, my darling girl!'

After the sharing of gifts, the evening meal, and tales of palace life, the excited boys finally fell asleep. Mother and daughter talked long into the night.

'I prayed hard that the curse would be averted. On the night of the full moon, I felt that your life had been saved, but until I saw you with my own eyes I could not be fully reassured.'

'Here I am, all in one piece, as you can see.'

'Will you return to the palace?'

'Yes, Mama. Princess Mirabella asked me to continue as her maid and accompany her to the new kingdom, but I declined. Miss Oleander has offered to train me in the arts of the apothecary. And... there is a young man...'

'Ah,' said her mother. 'I thought there might be, by the glow in your cheeks and the sparkle in your eyes. Tell me about him.'

'His name is Rolf. I will bring him to meet you when next I visit.'

'Does he return your love, this young man you speak of?'

'He does, Mama. You'll find him to be the kindest, most intelligent young man. He works in the kitchen, but one day I think he will be famous, for he is a botanist and a thinker by nature. He knows the names of birds and flowers, the ways of insects, so many interesting things. We wish to marry, but first we must save for a small cottage. We'll rear pigs for meat and for their joyous grunting; we'll grow plants for medicine as well as beauty. Perhaps in time we shall raise children, if God is willing.'

There came no words of reply, but Glory knew her mother's joy by the light in her eyes.

In case you're wondering what happened to the others: Arlo married Victoria, daughter of the blacksmith, and they became one of those couples that bicker about whether something happened on a Tuesday or a Friday. Lonely Jack's fortunes took a turn for the worse. Reading teacups didn't pay, so he resorted to more and more nefarious behaviours. He was arrested with stolen gold coins hidden in his beard, and imprisoned for ten long years. Dirk and Mrs Blossom never married, but indulged in generous amounts of cuddling whenever he delivered the honey. Elda was bequeathed a small inheritance from an uncle. She purchased an inn, The Silver Unicorn, which served the best pies in seven counties. Elda never married, believing that it was more hard work than she could be bothered with.

THE WRITER

It's always a bit odd when you finish writing a book. The writer is glad of it though. It's been a long road of many pages. Now it's time to send it out into the world, to let it take on a life of its own, unfolding like a lovely paper flower in someone else's imagination. The writer takes up her pen, pretends it's an elegant quill, dips it in Mirabella's golden inkpot, and with a lavish flourish she writes

The End

ACKNOWLEDGEMENTS

EARTFELT THANKS TO Sam Bodhi Field for his intelligence and encouragement.

Much appreciation to Robyn Bett, for giving (and telling) me the story of 'The Angry Princess' from *The Way of the Storyteller*, Ruth Sawyer (Penguin, 1977) and to Bruce Russell, for making the moussaka.

Warm thanks to Lydia, AKA Tamsin.

Thank you to Glenda Northey, Greg Ussher and Ella Manaia Ussher for research help.

Huge thanks to all the fabbo young people who email me, especially Taylor Jane, Jessica Howatson, Mary Scriven, and Madeleine Ballard. You brighten my life. I've stolen a thought or a half a line here or there from you. Please take it as a compliment. Also, please don't sue me. Special thanks to Madeleine Ballard for the acronyms and special days on page 128, and to Jessie Bray Sharpin for her last-minute, serendipitous help with a plot decision and a title.

The painting described on page 50 is by Hilary Herrmanne, and featured in *Inside Out* Magazine, (March/April 2009).

My tea readings were guided by *Secrets of Gypsy Fortune Telling* by Ray Buckland (Llewellyn Publishers, Minnesota, 1988).